HONEY BEE BLUES

HONEY BEE BLUES

A Novel

Mark Conkling

SUNSTONE
PRESS

SANTA FE

Sunstone books may be purchased for educational, business, or sales promotional use. For information please write: Special Markets Department, Sunstone Press, P.O. Box 2321, Santa Fe, New Mexico 87504-2321.

On the cover: "Sweet Nectar," photograph by Melodie A. Douglas

Book and cover design › Vicki Ahl
Body typeface › Constanis
Printed on acid-free paper
⊗
eBook 978-1-61139-550-1

Library of Congress Cataloging-in-Publication Data

Names: Conkling, Mark, 1941- author.
Title: Honey bee blues : a novel / by Mark Conkling.
Description: Santa Fe : Sunstone Press, [2018]
Identifiers: LCCN 2018002230 (print) | LCCN 2018006038 (ebook) | ISBN 9781611395501 | ISBN 9781632932211 (softcover : alk. paper)
Subjects: LCSH: Psychological fiction.
Classification: LCC PS3603.O535 (ebook) | LCC PS3603.O535 H68 2018 (print) | DDC 813/.6--dc23
LC record available at https://lccn.loc.gov/2018002230

WWW.SUNSTONEPRESS.COM
SUNSTONE PRESS / POST OFFICE BOX 2321 / SANTA FE, NM 87504-2321 /USA
(505) 988-4418 / ORDERS ONLY (800) 243-5644 / FAX (505) 988-1025

Dedicated
to
Bryan Michael Conkling

Hope is the thing with feathers
That perches in the soul,
And sings the tune—without the words,
And never stops at all...

—Emily Dickinson

Yesterday is dead and gone,
And tomorrow's out of sight,
And it's sad to be alone,
Help me make it through the night.

—Kris Kristopherson

Acknowledgments

*M*y heartfelt thanks to Vicky Chavez, Bob Guido, Kim Hamel, and Rochelle Williams for their editorial review and helpful comments. Special thanks to Patricia for her continued encouragement for my writing.

Preface

*H*ave you ever met a totally self-centered person? They're known as narcissists.

The most extreme form is a *narcissistic personal disorder*, like Dr. Jeff Corley, the protagonist in this novel. He has no empathy, no remorse, feels entitled, is deceptive and emotionally dependent, and projects a personality that is totally different from his true self. When provoked, such a person often abuses other people. What made him that way? Is there hope for change, for healing, for a normal life?

Honey Bee Blues tells the story of Jeff, his failed relationships with women, his self-deception, his despair, and his transformation. Rays of hope come into his life from spiritual forces in honey bees, a psychologist friend named Ben, a dental hygienist named Rachel, and the love of Emmy Lou, a childhood friend who he blinded when he was seven.

Although Jeff is difficult to like when you first meet him, he grows on you as he learns about himself and shows glimpses of recovery from his disorder. His ardent pursuit of lust and sex ruin relationships, and his immaturity seems fixed at about age thirteen. He is obsessive, rigid, and arrogant. He can't manage money. He lives on the edge of sanity, uses laughing gas for his anxiety, and he has a gambling addiction. Fortunately, his psychologist friend Ben helps him to understand his disorder, even though Jeff believes he's a superior man. It is a tough road for Jeff, and his journey leads to a failed suicide.

I wrote this novel because I believe there's always hope, even in the face of despair, and I wanted to show the recovery process of a deeply broken man. For years I've been fascinated by the destructive power of pride and the obsession to always be right. The philosopher Albert Camus said that "to believe you are absolutely right is the beginning of the end." The Greek idea of pride or Hubris has come to be known as the fountainhead of the seven deadly sins: pride, anger, lust, envy, greed, gluttony, and sloth or laziness. Pride lies at the heart of narcissism and drives Jeff Corley in his actions, and is the ultimate demon he must face. *Pride goes before destruction, a haughty spirit before a fall.* (Proverbs 16:18).

Honey bees are known for an inborn and instinctual force that creates the hive, their community, and their relationships. Honey bees serve one ideal, preservation of the hive and their community, the exact opposite of the destruction that comes from self-centeredness or pride. They are a fascinating form of life, exemplifying the power and sustenance of the natural world. We should learn from honey bees.

In Greek mythology, the character Icarus flew too close to the sun. He became so enthralled with his temporary ability to fly that he ignored his own limitations. His wings fashioned from wax and feathers melted and he dropped into the sea. All of us, to be healthy and whole, must at some time in our lives face our own limitations and ask for help. When this happens, a spiritual light comes on, and our spirits lead us into a state of hope. We come to believe that hope and love can overcome pride, and we become humble, seek out friendships and love, and dedicate ourselves to preserving our community—like the honey bees.

That's what happens to Dr. Jeff Corley. After incredible misfortunes, including a broken heart and unrequited love with a strange medicine woman, he finds a loving relationship and peace of mind. In the end, hope and love win out over pride. This is as it should be, don't you think?

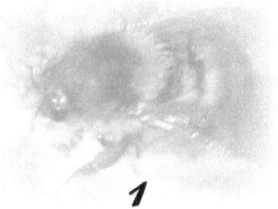

1

*R*oy and Janice Corley conceived Jeff at one-thirty under a full Buck Moon in July. They did it on the brown leather backseat of Roy's new, four-door, 1966 Oldsmobile parked in the Albuquerque Lutheran Church parking lot, the front windows open to a gentle breeze carrying the smell of honeysuckle. On this night of the rehearsal dinner for their wedding, Janice opened her womb to Roy for the first time. In the past, Janice had let Roy fool around some, but that was all. She was known as a faithful, moral and compassionate woman but her kind actions often masked selfish motives, a trait Jeff would inherit and later sharpen into an art. Janice was in her fertile time. She trembled, felt a quiver deep inside, and knew without question that Roy had hit the mark and she was pregnant, right there in the parking lot of the church full of friends who would gossip forever if they even suspected that the curled toes planted against the door window belonged to Janice Corley. Since the wedding was only a week away, this tiny tickle, soon to be named Jeffery Corley, would be known as their honeymoon baby. She grinned with delight, and wiggled her toes, knowing she would enjoy this secret for a lifetime. The coming of Jeffery changed their lives the day Roy pulled up to the hospital to pick up Janice and Jeff. "Well, Mom, let's take this little rug rat home."

Janice tipped her head, smiling. "Okay, Roy. You know from now on nothing will be the same. I'm afraid I won't have as much time for you."

"I know, but it's time to get on with our life. Come on. I've got stuff to do."

Jeff Corley began falling apart the day he came home. Genealogy might show that worms had eaten holes in his gnarled family tree, deep holes that later became fissures in his awareness, leading to a life fueled by spiritual pride, self-deception, and living on the edge.

Janice's bare legs moving in the shadow of the church steeple may have been the origin of Jeff's later risky behavior, just as Roy's eager lust may have been the beginning of Jeff's fickle ways—he would run through many girlfriends as he yearned for a wife who could love him dearly, a woman he imagined in exquisite detail, a happy woman who was evenly proportioned, even-tempered, even-minded, intelligent, gracious, attractive, sexy, and always eager to please him. Her presence would, of course, stop his constant turmoil, smooth the scars from his family tree, help him to relax, and to find his true self. And, she would fill the dark hole left in his heart when his childhood friend, Emmy Lou, moved away with her angry parents. His wife would hold him close and usher in his dream of a satisfied mind. A perfect woman and a peaceful mind. He knew he could find both.

The incessant greed that plagued his twenties and thirties was likely passed on from Janice's mother and the mother before her, both known for their avarice and shifty ways. Although moderated some by Janice's kindness, the genealogical force of greed ran underneath the remarkable beauty from Roy's mother, the beauty that attracted both men and women because of her oval face and large eyes, giving her the appearance of a harmless little fawn. Janice later mused that Jeff's charm and sweetness came from the honeysuckle fragrance mixed with his conception. No one knew for sure where he got his blond hair. It could have been Roy's great grandfather who had blond hair when he was young, but whose years of drinking and gambling turned his wrinkled skin to a yellow tone—his hair becoming a dishwater gray because of his life in prison.

Roy's eager swimmers and Janice's quick, responsive ovum somehow formed in Jeff a tenacious need to arrange things, to fret and worry about details, and to maintain an obsessive desire for control, character traits fully developed by his fifth birthday when he worried himself sick all night over a few minor bee stings. He had approached the beehives with innocent anticipation, alone and attracted by the loud buzzing sounds, but he moved too fast and several sentry bees dove under his collar and crawled up his shirt sleeves. They stung him as he ran toward the house, screaming. The swelling and throbbing produced horrible visions of lifelong, inescapable pain—fantasies that grew and made him toss and turn all night. In the morning, sleepless and blubbering, he shook his fist, shouted, ordering his father to move the beehives to behind the machine shed, farther from the house. Roy gritted his teeth, but after a cold stare from Janice, he took a breath and complied, thereby bestowing upon little Jeff his first taste of gratuitous power and control, feelings that arrived with an addictive force that filled in one of the wormholes in a branch of his family tree.

Also, that day marked the onset of one of Jeff's deepest fears and the emergence of his shadow. He became convinced that honey bees—bad ones—flew out into his future, pollinating the flowers of his misfortunes, and making his life miserable. He came to believe that all his problems came from bees or other people, never himself.

Jeff was a gorgeous baby with a sweet soul. Two days after Jeff's birth, the doctors, nurses, orderlies, and even people from the waiting room walked by the nursery to behold this charming boy who would be the next Gerber Baby, save that Janice didn't enter the Gerber contest because Roy saw it as female vanity, and he didn't want Jeff to turn out to be a pussy.

As Janice sat up and smoothed her skirt that night, a sudden hot twinge surged below her naval and deep inside, causing her to catch her breath and put her hands there. It was as though a hot flame had emerged from nowhere—a sudden cramp. Within a few moments, the heat diminished to a warmth that covered one side of her womb, the same flame that smoldered in Jeff like a buried fire in a landfill, hollowed out years of his life, and often caused Jeff to double over in pain—like that time thirty-six years later when he watched the jack of hearts fall on the blackjack table at the Casino.

The *ding-ding* noise of the slot machines decreased somewhat after two but the Sandia Casino in Albuquerque remained lit up and busy for the dedicated and the stalwart. Dr. Jeff Corley sat by himself at his lucky blackjack table. He had two cards, the two of clubs and the king of hearts.

"Hit me."

The dealer tossed out the jack of hearts. Jeff slapped his forehead. "Shit. Busted." The dealer scooped up fifty-four hundred dollars, Jeff's last chips. "Sorry, Dr. Corley."

Jeff held his breath as the heat rose in his belly. He grabbed a couple of antacid tablets from his shirt pocket and chewed them. "Damn. Thought that was going to be the big one." He stood up, bent over with his hand on his stomach, and steadied himself with the other hand on a leather-backed chair. He could smell his sweat under his arm.

"Are you sick?" The dealer motioned, and a waitress appeared with drinks.

"No, not sick. I'm pissed off. I should have seen that face card coming." He gulped down a full gin and tonic, rubbing his stomach. "It's just heartburn. Been bothering me a lot lately."

The dealer smiled. "Well, Dr. Corley, don't give up hope."

Jeff nodded and walked to the men's room and sat down on a toilet in a stall. He held his lowered head with both hands. *Tomorrow's Monday and they disconnect the phone. Can't run a dental office without a fucking phone. Registered mail from IRS. Payroll tax late....* He looked at his cell phone, but there was no one to call. On the wall to his left, someone had scrawled "always double down!" He drew back his right hand and slammed his open palm against the graffiti. Then he took off his right shoe, peeled back the insole, and took out a folded hundred-dollar bill, walked out to another blackjack table, and bought one-hundred dollars in chips—there's always tomorrow, and it was after midnight. It took until five, but he gathered up his winnings of about twelve-hundred dollars, enough for the phone bill and payment to the IRS. Close call, but he pulled it off. He was short of breath, his feet hurt, and he had a full day of appointments ahead of him: three crowns, two implants, and several estimates. He had to hurry to work.

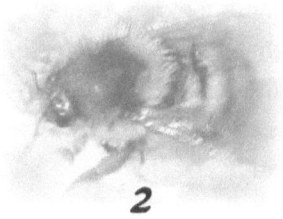

2

*J*eff's one-month-old wailing baby sister was the lone guest at his second birthday party. Mom tried to make the party pleasant, but after burying his hands in the cake, Jeff smeared frosting on his face and ears, licked his lips and hands, and then tottered into his bedroom by himself. By the time he was four, his brother Roy Junior was born, so the house was full of people—his busy, fussy mother who everyone called Mom, his nursing baby brother, his two-year-old sister Ida, and a gruff and tired father who came in after dark smelling of diesel fuel and wishing these rug rats hadn't arrived so close together. Jeff's mornings consisted of a steady stream of poopy diapers, the sour smell of milk and formula, and another bowl of oatmeal.

At six years of age, Jeff Corley's mind was in the throes of slipping away. His reveries dominated his time. He often found ways to be alone. After his chores, he would slip out the back door without being noticed, and that summer when school was out, he staked out a private place in an arroyo, two hundred yards from the house where he could not be seen and dug a cave. The following summer, he sawed off an old lock from an abandoned well house that was near the arroyo, drug out an old mattress from the machine shed, and filched one of his father's used tool boxes for a treasure chest. He stole a new lock and key from his father's parts drawer and claimed the well house as his domain. He kept the key in his shoe. There he hid out from the household mayhem and filled his tool box with dimes and quarters from his mother's purse and occasional dollar bills from his father's billfold. By the time he was seven, Jeff had created a different reality, a quiet place far away from noisy people, and a place where he could dream. His imagination planted seeds of a new persona, a child with aspirations of control, self-satisfaction, and isolation away from the indifference of his father, a strong little person focused on himself, his needs, and wanting people to like him. He was a good student, sought attention at school, and his teachers obliged. His quick responses, charming smile, and tendency to be entertaining without becoming rowdy, caught the eyes of teachers who were otherwise bored. He brought youthful zest to hum-drum places and turned work into surprise. He was an outwardly confident child who spent a lot of time admiring himself in mirrors and reflections in windows, perhaps to cope with his aching loneliness. The real Jeff Corley took a back seat to the handsome new boy in the mirror.

Had it not been for Emmy Lou Ketchum, Jeff could have slipped away into the unending reverie of his mind and the new Jeff would've taken over. Joe Ketchum, Emmy Lou's father, worked for Roy as a motor grader operator, and Margaret Ketchum, Emmy Lou's mother, was a friend of Mom's at church. Emmy Lou, Jeff's age, became a playmate who appeared every day after school and on into the summer. Jeff and Emmy Lou were always together, odd indeed because of Emmy Lou's bashful countenance. Emmy Lou's entry into the world was difficult—nearly a thirty-hour labor. When the nurse presented her to Margaret, she cuddled her to her breast and covered her head with a soft blanket, one of the only positions that made Emmy Lou comfortable. Even in infancy, she formed a habit of hunching her shoulders and tucking her head away from the activities around her, making her appear wary and timid. She didn't start talking until she was three and seemed reticent to play with other children, preferring instead to occupy herself with coloring books. Here she was, chasing around and laughing with Jeff, climbing dirt piles, following him around buildings, hiding out in the well house, and sitting together in the shade, sharing secrets. Jeff was taller than her by several inches. His height, her blond pigtails with pink ribbons, and her small rounded face made them look a little like older brother and sister, but they were the same age. She had a lot of stamina and could run faster than Jeff. He couldn't catch her no matter how hard he tried—unless she let him.

They had created trails, hiding places, and imaginary homes out by the well house and down the arroyos and their tributaries. They made up stories and acted them out. They sneaked food out of the house and made sandwiches for picnics. "They're like two peas in a pod," Mom would say, and Margaret was happy Emmy Lou had a friend because she was otherwise quiet and withdrawn, a trait shared by three generations of women in Margaret's family tree. In fact, had it not been for Jeff, Emmy Lou was on the path for a dark and introverted childhood. Never in his young, tiny life had Jeff cared about anyone or anything more than Emmy Lou. Sometimes he thought he would even die for her.

Emmy Lou was conceived in a shadow of fear and oppression just before dawn on a Friday morning. Joe had bragged to a friend on Thursday night that being married was great because you could just roll over anytime you wanted and tap right into it. Wives were compliant—that's why men got married. Margaret had always been a little wary of Joe, and she slept with her back to him, not because he ever hurt her, but because she somehow knew that he could. When she ventured to look full into his eyes, she felt a shiver run up her spine. Her gut told her that he carried something deep within him that she did not want to uncover. He drank often, laughed a lot, and worked hard. She could see that he might erupt if she crossed him or took charge of anything except the household. He was pushy that morning when he woke her up and rolled her over. Her full bladder made her shaky because she had to pee. Though unnerved and uncomfortable, she soldiered on, spread her legs, winced, and accommodated his heavy-handed poking, moving herself this way and that so he would be done as soon as possible, feeling chafed and used. She did not expect to get pregnant, just like her mother Louise had not expected to get pregnant with Margaret. They had both adjusted, settled into their compliant natures, and became dutiful parents, busying themselves with household tasks, mothering activities, and other chores that kept them at a safe distance from any intimate relationships with either of their husbands. Both Louise and Margaret developed quiet lives on the sidelines of their marriages, like silent spectators, rarely getting up on the stage. It was as though a generational memory had been passed on from mother to daughter, and now it settled on Emmy Lou as well.

It happened on a Saturday morning in August. Jeff and Emmy Lou had made up a game of "Indians," and Emmy Lou had painted Jeff's face with lipstick and mascara she took from her mother's bathroom. She laughed as she rubbed his cheek. "You look a little scary, but I like it."

"Put some dark streaks on my forehead, above my eyes, then under my eyes, okay?" He stooped down so she could reach. "Let's use the ashes."

She and Jeff had built a small fire, and Jeff had scraped up ashes on a flint arrowhead in preparation for painting her face. They had found that arrowhead three days ago far from the house. They cherished it because it was real and because they together discovered it. Jeff fashioned an arrow from a straight branch and tied on the arrowhead with fishing line from Roy's shop. They were down in the arroyo, out of sight.

Emmy Lou held the arrow close to the arrowhead. "Now hold still." She made four streaks with the ashes under Jeff's eyes, two on each side, and then two above each eye. "That looks good. My turn."

Jeff scooped out some dirt from the side of the arroyo and made a step for Emmy Lou. Jeff dipped the arrowhead into the ashes, waited for it to cool, and then made two straight lines on her upper right cheek. He took a small signal mirror out of his pocket. "Do you like that?"

Emmy Lou tipped her head and giggled. "That's great. Now the other side."

Jeff held her head with one hand and carefully spread ashes on her left cheek. Suddenly, the dirt step gave way, and she slipped and tumbled forward. The arrowhead plunged deep into her right eye. For a moment, they both froze, and then as blood started rushing out, Jeff laid her down on the dirt, pulled the arrowhead out, turned, and ran as fast as he could, screaming for help. As he ran by the bee hives on the way to the house, several sentry bees swooped on to his neck and face and stung him. By the time Mom had called 911, and the ambulance had arrived, Emmy Lou had passed out in a pool of her blood, and Jeff had returned to her side. The paramedics pushed Jeff out of the way and told him to go back to the house. When she got to the hospital, the doctor said the damage was too great to save her eye. Jeff came to dinner that night shaking and wiping his eyes. He held on tight to the arrowhead he had ripped off the shaft and buried deep in his pocket. Mom handed him tissues, and Roy glared at him. "Idiot, I've raised a freakin' idiot. What in the hell were you thinking? You blinded her. You're going to pay for this, mind my words."

"Is...is she blind?"

Mom put her hand on his. "Yes, in one eye. She'll have a glass eye after her surgery. I'm sorry, Jeff."

The next day, in the waiting room at the hospital, Mom and Roy offered to pay Emmy Lou's medical expenses since the Ketchum's did not have any health insurance. Roy didn't include coverage in Joe's wages. Although the estimate for costs was fifteen-thousand dollars, Joe and Margaret did not think it was enough—they also wanted twenty-five thousand for Emmy Lou's pain and suffering.

Mom put her hand on Margaret's shoulder. "Just let us take care of the expenses here, and we'll think about other ways we might help."

"I don't know what to say except she's going to have a glass eye. She's disabled forever. You should pay more. It's your stupid son's fault."

"Let's talk later," Mom said. "Give us a chance to think about it."

Joe didn't show up for work the next morning, and the motor grader was gone. Roy found it a half-mile away in a ditch with two flat tires, cut by the culvert Joe ran over. Joe had painted on the grader with red spray paint. "Fuck the Corleys I quit." Margaret sent copies of a scathing letter to everyone at the church and resigned her volunteer job in the kitchen, leaving Mom, as kitchen manager, in the lurch for an upcoming wedding rehearsal dinner. Her letter said, "We are moving. We can't stay here after what has happened to Emmy Lou. You should watch out for the Corley's. They're snakes. Leave us alone."

Mom and Roy argued most of that first night about Jeff's punishment.

"Roy, you know it was an accident. Let's have him write letters of apology to Emmy Lou and Margaret and Joe. Then he can come to church and pull weeds."

"Not enough. I'm going to whip Jeff's bare butt with my belt every day for a week."

"What good will that do? You're angry and embarrassed. For heaven's sake, it was an accident."

Mom stood up, gritted her teeth, and put her hands on her hips. "You leave him alone. Let's wait until this has cooled down. You should sleep on the couch tonight."

The next weekend Mom and Roy sat down with Jeff. All week long he had lived in fear, unable to sleep, awaiting his fate in a swirl of childhood confusion, his face still swollen from bee stings. He knew he didn't mean to do anything bad, but because of him, Emmy Lou was blind in one eye. Finally, they agreed. Jeff would weed at the church, help Mom with chores, and would work at home for Roy until he had worked off the cost of new tires for the grader. Roy whipped him one time with his belt. "You've got to learn to think. I won't have a stupid son," Roy said. "Now pull up your pants and quit sniveling." He made Jeff shovel and spread gravel along the long driveway every day after school for a week. Jeff hung his head and worked, his seven-year-old body slowing to a snail's pace until Roy shouted, "Hey, pick it up over there. You're slacking."

That week, Jeff tried to help Mom with the beehives. She dressed Jeff in a suit with a hat and net. She taped the oversize pants around his ankles with duct tape, gave him a pair of thick leather gloves, and tightened his collar with twine. Jeff looked like a little beekeeper swimming in a wrinkled and baggy suit.

"Just stay calm," Mom said. "They won't sting you if you're quiet. I don't think we'll need to use any smoke if we move slowly." Jeff tripped on one of his pants cuffs. As Mom helped him up, several bees managed to get inside his collar in the back, and one got up one of his sleeves. They stung him at the same time, and he shouted and flapped his arms, which stirred all the bees in the hives. Although two of the hives were friendly, the third hive erupted with a vengeance, and he and Mom had to run to the house and spray themselves with the hose. Each time he tried to help he got stung—three weekends in a row—no matter how Mom taped him up. It was as though sentry bees had memorized the smell of Jeff's skin and flew to him like the nectar in purple sage. Jeff hated those bees and would not eat the honey Mom harvested. She tried to get him to help crank the centrifuge, but he refused to help. In fact, when no one was looking, from a distance he would throw rocks at the hives and then run to the old well house and hide before the bees came after him. Bee stings felt to him like punishment for his stupidity, for blinding Emmy Lou—they hurt deep into his little heart, as deep as hurt could go.

Emmy Lou and her parents moved away before Jeff had a chance to apologize. Mom made him mail her a letter, but it was returned. For months, in his dreams, Emmy Lou's eye would swoop up close and look at him through tears and blood, the arrowhead still embedded. He never told anyone. After repeated nightmares, Jeff took on massive shame, and his posture changed as if he was carrying a rucksack on his shoulders. Emmy Lou's memory was bound up with the arrowhead he kept in his pocket. Jeff often rubbed it like a worry stone. He became more of a loner and his active imagination continued to shape an alternate person, a boy who was smart, well-liked, confident, and who could control most everything around him, a boy who would take care of himself in all circumstances, a quiet boy who could be charming, devious, selfish, and detached from other peoples' feelings and who was not afraid to take chances. Pride blanketed his fear of bees, and self-deception attached to his mind. He often laid on the quilts in the well house and imagined that he was someone else and lived somewhere else and didn't have a sister or brother. He thought of all the things he could be and all the ways he could be, and he made his imagination into his best friend. Sometimes he lost himself in reverie, a hypnogogic state of mind where he found comfort in drifting away from the real world.

Maybe he would be famous. Maybe everyone would like him. Maybe he would have everything he wanted and even live with a different family. Maybe he would never again feel ashamed. Maybe he should always think of himself first, no matter what his mother said. Yes, he was important and should come first, and he didn't care how other people felt if he got what he wanted. He'd return to the moment when he heard his mother ringing the dinner bell on the front porch. Jeff would hustle himself back through his arroyo trails and wander into the mud room, wash his hands, and appear in the kitchen a few minutes before his father came in from the workshop. He kept his head down while eating and muttered short answers when asked questions. A fog seemed to hang over his father, a gray mist through which Roy often looked askance at Jeff because he lived with the continuing worry that Jeff would never measure up. After dinner, after a bath and brushing his teeth, he went to bed with a flashlight and read comic books under the covers—Captain Marvel, Superman, the Green Hornet, Batman—imagining that he had superpowers, that he could, at will, escape the dreams of Emmy Lou's eye and become the new boy—that remarkable boy that stood tall while breaking loose from the shroud of shame around the old child he left behind.

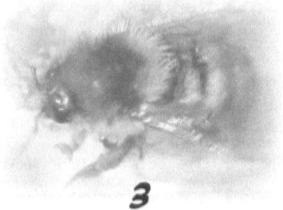

3

I did another all-nighter at Santa Ana Casino and walked out in the early dawn with seventeen-hundred dollars, enough for the month's rent. It was getting harder, but my luck was still with me, and my mind was sharp. I could count cards with the best of them, and I moved around among tables until I found a hot one. The luck of the table and the skill of my mind kept my creditors at bay. It was too late to sleep, so I drove on Interstate 25 to the Embassy Suites to have breakfast. I washed my face and combed my hair in the men's room, sat down in the dining room, ordered a cheese, spinach, and mushroom omelet, and put eye drops in both eyes. Two quick cups of coffee perked me up. I was ready to go to work.

As a medical professional, I'm quite circumspect, but that morning, maybe because I was so tired, I stared wide-eyed and directly at her—the woman by the cash register in the tight, white spaghetti-strap, jersey shirt, a striking woman whose perky right nipple was at least three inches above her left one, both nipples perched on full breasts. Her right eyebrow raised in the same proportion above her left eyebrow, and her puffy smile raised on the right in the same way. I even tipped my head so my gaze would match her nipples, about a twenty-two degree angle. Disturbing, fascinating.

I forced myself to look away as a large man came up behind her and circled her waist with his hands as she leaned back into his blue blazer and folds of his hefty torso, her nipples becoming even more erect as the air conditioning cycled on, sending a blast of chilly air from a vent nearby.

"Your table is ready. Come this way." The hostess sat them at the table next to me and handed them menus. The woman in the white shirt turned to look out the window at the rising sun, crossing her arms, then turned back, catching me staring. *Busted.* I'll bet I'm not the first. People must have wondered before. I mean, she brought it on herself with that shirt. Why didn't she wear a bra and try to even herself out? Couldn't she pull up the low one? How hard is that?

No—and that's the interesting part, as I found out later—she didn't care. She knew she was uneven, and she didn't care. I remember thinking there's such a thing as order and symmetry in the universe. The least she could do is get that eyebrow fixed. She looked like she was finding fault with everything. With a little practice, she could smooth out her smile. She could train those muscles. How hard is that?

She told me later she took pride in her unevenness. It was part of her unique identity. Then I found out from hours of listening that it also characterized her mind—uneven body, uneven mind, a mind that trusted science, consulted astrologers, and memorized bird whistles; a mind that thought logical thoughts and imagined Victorian dresses and lustful sighs in romance novels; a mind that could rapidly shift attention from flu shots to baby showers to quilting to baking cookies to new shoes to an orgasm—unevenness. My psychologist friend Ben would call it attention deficit disorder, but it was the way of the world for Michelle Peterson, a twenty-nine-year-old registered nurse from Indianola, Iowa. She was a woman already having doubts about her new marriage, a union born on the Internet and consummated in front of a forty-two-inch TV upstairs in the Embassy Suites. She told me later that her husband Henry propped his neck up with a pillow and kept his eye on *Law and Order* as she sat astride him, moving slowly, watching her romantic dreams flutter away in the flicker of reflected faces of lawyers on the wall. I'll be he didn't even notice her uneven nipples swaying. Christ, I would. Given a chance, I'd hold her breasts and maybe even them up a little. I mean, wouldn't you?

Michelle told me these things first at Starbucks and over the rest of the day, while often dabbing her tears with a brown recycled napkin. It was a chance encounter with strained intimacy, though maybe fate drove the intimacy. Why me? Why did she overflow with so much to say? I don't know how I had the patience for this except that I felt strong having a little power over her.

Michelle Peterson was conceived early one Thursday morning on a farm in Iowa in a barn in the hayloft on a quilt spread out on a pile of hay. Cows were mooing below wanting to be milked. Her mother Maryann had pulled the quilt off the clothesline as she walked to the barn with her father Lawrence, looking at him with a glint in her eye.

"The next couple of days are good times," she said. "I mean if you want to have a baby."

They scurried up the ladder, and she spread out the quilt. Lawrence took off his overalls and undershorts. He grinned. "Okay, those cows can wait."

Maryann raised her pink housecoat, kicked off her rubber boots, settled into a comfortable position and welcomed him with open arms. Lawrence had a tough time keeping his balance on the sloped hay pile, but he jammed his right elbow into the quilt-covered hay for support. They proceeded among the sounds of rustling alfalfa and insistent mooing. The sweet smell of Maryann's mint toothpaste and lavender bath soap overpowered the wafting odor of cow manure. Whispered words of love drowned out the mooing.

"Wow, that ought to do it," she said as he moved to the side, out of breath. "Let's wait here a minute." She put both legs up in the air and held them there with her hands behind her knees. "I want to make sure this takes."

Michelle was their first and only child—strong, capable, smart—and some would say overprotected, spoiled rotten and not too swift at judging people, features from her grandmother on her father's side. Grandmother Bertha was also an only child, and she married an itinerant farm worker who drank himself to death before Lawrence had turned seven. She raised him as a single mother on a small farm nearby and depended on neighbors at harvest time. She gardened, butchered, taught him how to be self-sufficient, and got dentures before she was forty because of her habit of grinding her teeth at night. She never married again and devoted herself to singing in the choir, cooking, and leading a women's group at the First Baptist Church. Michelle's Grandmother Agnes on Maryann's side was a self-styled artist and made crafts of all kinds that she sold on consignment in the general store. She loved bold colors and made purple angels, red kittens, and chartreuse puppies from cornstalks, and she made blue chickens, yellow goats, and orange cows from corncobs. Her figurines were charming and sold well to passersby as mementos of the farm community. Neighbors said Agnes was daft, but she was a good mother to Maryann, and she laughed out loud at her husband Henry's jokes. Agnes was an artful gossip—her news coming in whispers—and she loved to run naked in the rain at night. If it was raining in the daylight, she wore her blue cotton nightgown. She didn't seem to care if a neighbor saw her. It was her body and her rain, and they could just get over it.

Michelle, unabashed about her nipples, and wanting to get past that topic, was quick to point out that no human body is symmetrical. "One side is always different from the other. Have you ever looked in the mirror? Check your ears, your eyebrows, your nostrils. They are different. Look at your chest. Your nipples are different, too. You're a man—you know about unevenness, for heaven's sake. One of your testicles is larger than the other, and it hangs down further. Right? Watch who you're calling uneven. Look at the physics of things. You don't find symmetry until you get to the atomic level, and even there it is an elusive search. I don't understand the problem. I'm uneven, and people can just deal with it. Why the hell do you care? I'm tired of people trying to match everything up, make things even."

"Yes, I know, but come on, haven't you heard of the music of the spheres? The essence of the universe is ordered. Planets do have orbits, and mathematics works well for space travel. I mean, the law of nature is there, and it's our job to keep it from running down, don't you think? We don't need to add to disorder. And for sure, we don't have to feature it. Bodies aren't perfect, but at least we have some standards. We can maintain things, fix things, whiten teeth, correct overbites, and strive for perfection. Being odd is one thing, but flaunting it is something else."

We first encountered each other standing in line at Starbucks on Friday as she ordered a nonfat latte. As she turned, she stumbled on my foot and spilled her drink. "Could you please move? You're crowding me."

She looked up at me as I stepped back. "Sorry. Can I help you with that?" I grabbed a handful of napkins, crouched down beside her, and started sopping up the decaf latte. My face bumped hers. I smelled her lavender perfume and herbal shampoo. Her eyebrows furrowed, then the right one rose again, spring-ing back to its arched position. I held up her cup, nodding at the barista to fix another latte. She stood, and I turned to face her. "Hello, I'm Jeff Corley. I'm sorry. I didn't mean to make you spill your latte." I smiled. "I remember seeing you at the Embassy Suites in the restaurant."

She extended her hand. "I'm Michelle Peterson." The barista gave me her replacement latte and motioned to my Americano. I picked it up with my other hand.

"I'll take this to your table, okay?" We walked to a corner coffee table by two overstuffed chairs. I put the cup down, standing there, shifting on my feet.

"Would you like to join me?" she asked.

"Sure. Are you from here—from Albuquerque?"

"Well, sort of. I'm here on my honeymoon."

"Oh, maybe I shouldn't be sitting here."

"Henry—my husband—is taking a nap. I'm out shopping. It's okay. Thanks for helping me clean up that spill."

All I did was listen, or look like I was listening, that's all. I listened to Michelle at Starbucks for an hour, and then we walked through the Nob Hill shopping area, and I listened while we walked past the gift shops and restaurants. Then we walked outside and sat on a park bench, and I listened there. Then we sat on the grass, and I listened some more. I didn't ask her a single thing. I've learned, however, if you lean forward and listen to a woman, she'll tell you a lot of interesting things, which can also be a problem if she needs things. There are some things I'd rather not know, so I've learned when to stop listening and to take charge before she spoils everything. But sitting there on the grass, out of nowhere, she told me about her new husband watching *Law and Order* while she yearned for romance and tried to have what she called a honeymoon feeling—the shadows of the TV program on the wall defeated her attempt. I nodded my head, watched her animated hand gestures, her swinging auburn ponytail, and her tired green eyes, and imagined her straddling and moving up and down, uneven breasts swaying.

"Can you imagine? He's gentle, smart, and successful with his insurance business, never been married before, adores me and loves to travel. He's overweight, but he said he's willing to change his diet to match mine and to start walking every day. He's a moral man, he took me to his church, we dated for eight months, and I respected his wishes to wait—you know, wait until we were married, before we had sex—but *Law and Order*? Jesus Christ, I can't believe he was watching TV over my shoulder. Waiting was a mistake, that's for sure." Both her eyebrows rose, and her cheeks flushed. I nodded in agreement. I couldn't imagine watching TV with this woman sitting on me, yearning for me. I'll bet that eyebrow comes down when she closes her eyes. She looked at her phone, flushed, and slapped her hand on her forehead. "I can't believe I've been talking for three hours, to a stranger."

"I'm not a stranger anymore. It seems like you needed to talk."

Both cheeks turned pink. "Well, I guess that's right. Now I'm downright embarrassed. What about you, Jeff? Where are you from?"

"Albuquerque. I'm a dentist. Solo practice."

"Oh, I have a couple of friends in Albuquerque. They work at Presbyterian

Hospital. We went to nursing school together in Denver."

"So, you sometimes visit Albuquerque?"

"Now and then. I like it here, but we live in Portland."

"I was born here—plan on staying."

"You're young. Have you been a dentist long?"

"Not that young. I'm thirty-six, and I finished my degree in two thousand one. I've been practicing here for five years."

"Do you have a family?"

"No. I'm single." I grinned at her. "I'm available in case you hear of someone who's looking."

She stood up, and we strolled back through the market. We stopped for a moment beside the fresh rainbow trout on a bed of lettuce on crushed ice. The fish was on his stomach. I pointed and grinned. "That trout's eyes seem pretty even to me. Look like little headlights."

She bent down, studying the eyes. "Nope, they're a little off." She turned and smiled, extending her hand. "It was good to meet you, Jeff. I've got to get back to the hotel."

"It was great to meet you too. Maybe our paths will cross again. Who knows what the future holds for people like us."

"People like us?"

"You know, lonely people, people who have chance encounters. Maybe it means something."

She lifted both eyebrows evenly. "Lonely people?"

My face flushed. "Yeah...I gather both of us are lonely."

She looked down and folded her hands. "I think...I think I'm going to end my marriage before it goes any further."

My eyes opened wide. "Wow, on your honeymoon?"

"No, I'll wait until we get back to Portland."

"What will you tell him?"

"I'll tell him the truth. I just don't think we're a match."

She turned and walked away, chin up, arms swinging by her side.

Best as I could tell unless her tight blue jeans shaped her up, her hips were symmetrical. Looked like they matched. Cheek to cheek. Nice and even.

That was the last time I thought about Michelle until May 2005 when she showed up at my office wanting a crown for her upper right first bicuspid, the same side as her raised eyebrow.

4

*J*eff met Ben Ortega, soon to become his only male friend, in an Introductory Psychology class Fall semester at the University of New Mexico in 1995 when Jeff had to take a Psychology class as a freshman. Ben was a graduate student teaching the introductory course and had completed all coursework in clinical psychology. He was working on his dissertation on personality disorders and would have his PhD and license by June 1996. In the meantime, he taught two sections of Intro to Psych, and informally counseled students at the UNM Medical Clinic. He did intake interviews and recommended treatment plans. His mentors discovered Ben's remarkable perceptiveness, and often let him counsel students through ten or twelve sessions and write diagnostic reports that he later incorporated into his dissertation. Ben had memorized the DSM-IV and understood symptomatology.

Ben is tall, easy going, and friendly. In his late twenties, his hair is prematurely gray, and he keeps it short. He wears glasses, and his blue eyes and subtle smile suggest that he sees more than most people and that he reads people well, features that add considerable competence to his work in counseling. Ben lived in the country north of Albuquerque in an adobe house on two acres in Algodones. His neighbor had a beautiful orchard with rows of apple, peach, and apricot trees. Ben kept three bee hives, and in addition to nectar from the native wildflowers, the bees were pollinators for the orchard. Peacefulness shows on Ben's face, which tends to draw people to him, to open to this strong, harmless presence. Ben cared about helping people, especially men. On his application to the Clinical Psych graduate program, to the question "Why do you want to be a Clinical Psychologist?" He wrote, "to help men find relief from their psychic pain and suffering." That answer contributed in large measure toward his acceptance into the program and a graduate teaching assistantship.

Ben specialized in anxiety disorders, addictions, obsessions, and personality disorders—especially narcissistic personality disorders. He believed that men need to discover who they are, free themselves from the dark forces of dysfunction and resentment, and live authentically with purpose and courage, always challenging themselves with goals and dreams, always mindful of the shadow deep within. Like Jeff, Ben was born and raised in Albuquerque.

Ben's mother and father, Rosalina and Charles Ortega, conceived Ben peacefully, eagerly, and quietly on their second honeymoon in a hotel in Albuquerque when Charles came home from Vietnam for a leave over Christmas, 1971. They had been apart for over a year, so the weekend was spent in bed, like their honeymoon. Early on Sunday morning, Charles awoke to Rosalina stroking him, and then to her laying on top of him, whispering quiet little breath groans. She put her mouth to his ear. "Do you think we should have a baby?"

He hugged her close. "Yes, of course."

She began moving. "Okay, then—no condom. We'll see what happens."

Ben was a fine baby. He had a full head of brown hair, blue eyes, and a little smile that charmed every passerby in the nursery. Charles only got to see him a few times. He returned to Viet Nam to help protect the embassy in Da Nang but was killed by a supply truck just as the war ended in 1973.

Orlando, Ben's grandfather on his father's side, was also a charmer. Rumors suggested that he had scores of lady friends, but only one who he loved, Ben's grandmother, Philomena, a gentle, stalwart, and devoted wife who believed in the sanctity of marriage and taking care of her man. Orlando basked in Philomena's care and never strayed.

Loren, his grandmother on his mother's side, met his grandfather Anthony at choir practice for a Christmas Cantata at St. Mary's Catholic Church in Roswell, New Mexico. After having dinner with her mother and father, their courtship progressed, and they were married one year later. Grandfather Anthony was a gentleman from the old school and was taken aback, although delighted when he discovered on their honeymoon that Loren was a wild woman in bed. At first, he was shaken by her uninhibited ways, but soon it became his hidden secret that he wore on his pink cheeks. Overall, the family tree produced a good measure of love and passion that eased Ben into the world, arming him for the hard journey ahead.

When Ben was seven, Rosalina married a widower named Henry who lived two blocks away. He later revealed that he didn't like children, although he would tolerate Ben if he were well behaved. Henry sold his house soon after they were married, and moved into Rosalina's house. Ben's father's military life insurance was substantial, and Rosalina had paid off the mortgage. During the next year, Ben took a back seat to the nurturing care of his mother who was now required to pay substantial attention to Henry. Ben remained confused and angry throughout his childhood, wondering why his mom spent so much time with Henry, why he was so selfish, why she and Henry went out so often, why he was usually left out, why they always drove new cars, why his stomach always felt queasy, and why his eyes looked dark in the mirror.

Henry and Ben never did connect. Ben lived a quiet life, a stranger in his own home. He stayed away, hung out with friends, and focused on becoming an excellent student. Often Henry and Rosalina didn't even realize that Ben was not home in his room. He covered up his resentment with good grades, awards, and dreams of escaping Henry's harsh words and scrutiny. His time alone became more important, and his fantasy life grew into reveries of ways he could disappoint his mother—perhaps even teach her a lesson about her mindless abandonment and overdone allegiance to that asshole Henry. When he was despondent, he would fantasize about smacking Henry with a baseball bat and bringing home a prostitute to meet his mother and introduce her as his fiancé.

Just after his eighteenth birthday, Ben started at the University of New Mexico on a full academic scholarship. One Saturday in August as he was packing his things to move out, he paged through an old Bible his father had bought for him when he was an infant. In the middle, in Psalms, he found a letter written on thin airmail tissue paper. Someone had opened the envelope.

> Dear Ben,
>
> I'm writing this letter because I must go back to the war. In case anything happens to me, I put away money for you—gold coins. They are in a safe deposit box at First National Bank, worth about one-hundred thousand dollars. When you are eighteen, go there and find vice president George or his wife, Maria. I trusted them with the safe deposit box key. I hate to say it, but I don't think you can trust your mother with money, especially if she finds another man. She'll want to please him, and he'll walk all over her. I hope I can get home soon and you won't even see this letter.
>
> Love, Dad

Ben threw the Bible into a suitcase, slammed it shut, marched into the living room and put his hands on his hips. His lips quivered.

"Mother, did you open that letter from my dad?"

Henry scowled, and Rosalina stood up. "Letter?"

Ben clenched his teeth. "Yes, the letter in my Bible about the gold coins."

She dropped her head and put her hands together. Henry stood up, stepped in front of her, and faced Ben with a cold stare. "Raising a child is expensive. We needed that money for your expenses—you know, school, braces, medical costs, clothing, food—things like that."

Ben looked at his mother, but she wouldn't meet his eyes.

"The banker knew the gold coins were for me."

Henry smiled. "He was aware that they were for the family. You are a minor, so we set up a trust. Your mother is the trustee."

His face reddened. "How much is left for college?"

His mother shook her head. "I'm so sorry."

Ben took a breath, made fists with his hands, but left them at his side. "I guess this is goodbye."

Henry extended his hand. "Be sure and check in and let your mother know how you're doing."

Ben ignored his hand, turned, and walked to his room to gather his things. He would never return, except one time late at night the following winter. On the anniversary of his father's death, his palms sweating and his stomach churning, Ben slashed all the tires on Henry's new BMW and spat on the windshield. *That was my money. I'll slash the tires if I want.*

Although the class was large, Jeff's blond hair, light brown eyes, broad white smile, and bright presence made him stand out. He often slipped in just as class started, followed by laughing young women he had engaged in conversation. After a couple of tests, Ben was impressed with Jeff's outstanding performance and wrote on his test that he would like to see him in his office. Jeff obliged.

"Your test scores are way above the norm, Jeff. Remarkable I'd say. You must like Psychology."

"I do well in all my classes. Psychology is just one of them."

"So, then, you must like college."

"It's a pain, but I can't get into dental school unless I have a science degree and a high GPA. Most of my classes are easy. I'm brilliant, but I can't test out of subjects until after my freshman year."

"Dental school is your goal?"

"Yes, I've always wanted to be a dentist, ever since I was little."

"Gosh, have you ever wondered why?"

"Yes, and I've got it figured out. There's something structural, permanent, and beautiful about the human face and jawline. It is the foundation for beauty in women and strength in men. Our jaw-lines, our teeth, our smiles are what makes movie stars and models, the best of humanity."

"What about the folks who aren't so beautiful?"

"I can help them, and people are willing to pay for beauty. I want to go into cosmetic dentistry. You'd be surprised what I will be able to accomplish. Have you ever met a snaggle-toothed woman who has high self-esteem?"

"Can't say that I have."

"Well, there aren't any. When your teeth are ugly, that's how you feel—ugly."

"You have high test scores, and you've identified your life purpose, yet you're only about twenty. How did you get to be so intelligent so young?" Ben rested his jaw on his upturned palm.

"I think I was just born that way, and I've focused on maximizing my abilities."

"Sounds like you have a lot of self-confidence. You must have come from a good family."

"No. My mother was always busy, and my father never thought much of me. I'm a self-made man, and I've had to put together a life with my own resources. I have self-confidence because of what I've made of myself."

Ben smiled. "Your essay responses indicate you understand people. Is that a gift or have you developed the ability?"

"For me to get ahead and stay competitive, I had to learn how to read people and how to step out in front. It's not difficult once you get a feel for it. People are transparent. But why are you asking me these things? Are you trying to steer me into a Psych major? That's not going to happen. Psychology is too shallow."

"No, I'm not trying to steer you. It's quite simple. Intelligent people are interesting to me. I just wanted to get to know you. Maybe we should have lunch sometime."

Jeff tilted his head and grinned. "Sure. That would be okay. I've often wondered what makes psychologists tick."

"I have to admit, Jeff. My motives are mixed. I'm getting close to finishing my dissertation. Men with overwhelming self-confidence are part of my studies. Do you see yourself as a little superior to the others in the class?"

"That should be obvious. You said it yourself. I'm remarkable. Always have been."

"How about Wednesday at the student union, say about twelve thirty?"

Jeff stood up and extended his hand. "Okay, I'll meet you there. Maybe you can learn something from me for your dissertation."

Ben shook his hand. "Thanks for coming by. See you Wednesday."

As Jeff turned to walk out, Ben smiled and looked down at his desk, shaking his head. Classic. Perhaps he would learn something. Jeff reminded him of some of the drones in his hives. He expected the world to feed and care for him.

On Wednesday, they met for lunch and continued the conversation. There was a mix of mutual curiosity and natural attraction between them. Jeff was somewhat trusting, and Ben let down some of the boundaries between student and teacher, unusual behavior for both.

Ben put down his fork. "What do you like to do in your spare time?"

Jeff smiled. "I like to go to the Casino, to movies, and meet eligible young women. I'm particular. I want perfection."

"You like to gamble?"

"Yeah, some. I like blackjack because I can keep track of the cards. I usually win."

"Do you have any pets?"

"I do. One little bird named Budgey. His chirping and twitter brighten up my apartment. Do you have any pets?"

"No, Jeff. Not really pets. But I am a beekeeper. I've got three hives, wild-flowers, and an orchard next door. I'll bring you a jar of my honey."

"I don't eat honey, and I hate bees."

"Really? What's that about?"

"Mother made me help with our bee hives when I was little. I got stung a lot." Jeff shivered. "The bees always got in my clothes. I couldn't get away."

"Sorry to hear that. Bees have a lot to teach us about life."

"All they've taught me is pain. They make me miserable when I'm around them."

"Okay, enough about bees. What about movies? Did you see *Forrest Gump*?"

"Sure did. Won the Academy Awards you know—best picture and best actor."

"Tom Hanks was great—versatile," Ben said. "And so was Gary Sinise. Lieutenant Dan was upset because Forrest saved his life—he wanted to die in battle—but then he becomes Forrest's first mate on the shrimp boat and forgives him. I like watching men transform like that. Do you?"

"Oh, I guess, but Jenny was my favorite. Earthy. Deep down sexy. She had faults, though. Do you think she died from AIDS?"

"Yes. Or HEP-C. She was living loose."

"Well, she turned me on anyway. The sex scene with Forrest was great."

"Yeah. Forrest was so innocent, and Jenny was so worldly—charming."

"Poor Forrest. He didn't know what hit him, but in the morning, he sure did."

"Have you seen the new movie *Seven*?"

"No, is it good?"

"Supposed to be. It just came out. Kevin Spacey is a serial killer, and Brad Pitt and Morgan Freeman are detectives. It's dark. The plot explores the seven deadly sins with seven murders. Hey, would you like to go?"

Jeff tilted his head. "Do you mean we go together?"

"Sure. We could take in the Saturday matinee."

"I don't know...someone might think we're gay."

Ben laughed. "I don't believe so. It's a psychological thriller so we can go as a class assignment. I could meet you there. You could write an essay for extra credit."

"Okay, I'll have it figured out in a heartbeat."

Ben opened a newspaper on his desk. "Matinee is at one thirty-five at Cinemark Movies Eight. I'll meet you at the ticket office about one?"

They stood up. A tall brunette walked by and smiled at Jeff. He watched her sauntering hips walk away, then nodded. "Hey, check it out."

Ben smiled. "See you Saturday. We can go for coffee after."

The movie was intense and dark and captivating. The serial killer had killed seven people in symbolic ways that showed the power of the seven deadly sins that reside in hearts of humanity, the power of evil incarnate.

They sat down in a nearby Starbucks. Ben shook his head. "That was intense. I'll never forget that movie. How about you?"

"Tough stuff. I'm never going to overeat again."

"Yeah, and the pound of flesh from the lawyer—greed personified. What did you think of the woman?"

"The one sliced up by lust?"

"No, the disfigured one, the Model. The murder that depicted pride."

"That was an easy choice—she had to choose between calling for help and being disfigured or committing suicide by taking pills. She made the right choice."

"You think?"

"For sure. Attractive people would rather be dead than ugly—I know I would."

This friendship was odd. It began with Ben's curiosity, but then became a regular companionship that peaked Jeff's interest as well. Ben opened a private practice near the University campus after graduation. Jeff tested out of two years of undergraduate coursework, was admitted to dental school, excelled, and graduated at the top of his class. He opened his private practice in 2001 in the Northeast Heights in Albuquerque with a bank loan—a professional loan to an up-and-coming cosmetic dentist—a self-made man. Jeff and Ben spent time together throughout all the changes and helped each other move furniture into their offices. Jeff failed at many relationships during those eight years, and Ben was there to listen, to be Jeff's friend, and to offer advice on emotional intelligence, self-awareness, and empathy for others. The information fell on Jeff's deaf ears, ears filled with the waters of self-deception that for years masked the inner turmoil and anxiety that had become Jeff's companions. Psychology was bunk, beneath his superior mind, but Ben was a good friend, his only male friend. He had no one else to talk to, at least no one else he could trust except for Rachel. Throughout those years, Jeff never visited Ben at his home in Algodones, nor did Ben go to Jeff's apartment. They kept their friendship semi-professional.

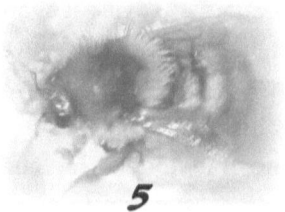

5

*R*achel Curry was Jeff's only woman friend. She ran his dental office and watched out for him. Theirs' was a strange relationship, defined for the most part by the mutual attraction of their troubled paths and by sheer serendipity. Jeff didn't understand the feelings he had for her because they were weak and fleeting, like quick, little cramps at the bottom of his heart. She had a long stride, and her red hair and vague green eyes seemed mysterious every time he looked at her, as though she was a woman inside a kaleidoscope, sending out flashes of changing lights.

Rachel was conceived from behind on an elevator in her father's office building at three on a Wednesday afternoon in December in 1985. Her father and mother were on the way up to his office. He stopped the elevator between the third and fourth floor, grinned, motioned his head toward her mother, slowly turned her toward a corner, raised her skirt past her protesting hands, pulled her pantyhose down, grabbed both hips, and pulled her to him with a tight grip. She looked back over her shoulder. "Do we have to do this now?"

"Yes, now. Fun, don't you think?"

She put her hands up on the two walls, relenting. She leaned her head down toward the corner, pushed back, and waited until he finished and jerked away. She straightened her clothes, turned, pushed the up button on the elevator, and began making a mental list of the Christmas cards she needed to address and mail as the door opened on the fifth floor.

He took her elbow and escorted her into the law offices of Curry and Associates. "I'm glad you could come and visit."

"Just leave me alone. Right now, I'm pissed off. You can be a real ogre, you know."

Rachel's red hair came from her great grandmother, the only other redhead in the gene pool. Dark red in some places, streaks of orange in others, and when she shook her head, she looked like a flame. Her great grandmother was emotionally labile and uneven, a trait inherited by Rachel—her temper was unpredictable, even to herself, and she often gritted her whitened teeth behind a full smile and her pink complexion. She didn't share her emotional state with others, but when riled, her irritation swept over her whole face, making her appear like a chubby-faced three-month-old crying baby.

Rachel was a little short for her full figure. She would have been taller had it not been for Shorty, her great, great grandfather, an anomalous short offshoot from the rest of the family tree. Back then, whispered remarks suggested he had not been conceived by the tall father he claimed, but rather he was the result of a dalliance with a short neighbor man who stayed at home and worked in his garden during the day. His circumspect sisters did not let the rumor go far, but insider speculation followed the family all the way to Rachel, and her father teased Rachel's mother with remarks like, "looks like the gardener planted seeds everywhere."

As far back as anyone could remember, Rachel's gray-green eyes first appeared with Rachel's great-grandmother, Minnie, on her father's side, and the combination of red hair and gray-green eyes did not appear until Rachel was born.

Her grandmother was a strong woman and spent her lifetime volunteering for the Salvation Army and other rescue organizations. Rachel's mother, Sandra, was an only child and lived in the shadows of her busy and often absent mother. Her father was an accomplished lawyer and had a way of towering over her and her mother. He was powerful, mysterious, handsome, and didn't talk much with Rachel. One of Rachel's friends at school told her that her father thought Rachel's dad was shifty, a feature Rachel herself displayed as small child by taking money from her mother's purse when she was drinking in the evenings—almost four-hundred dollars by the time she was eight, the year her mother left in the middle of the night on a Friday in September. Rachel was surprised to see her father sitting at the kitchen table in the morning.

He smiled and motioned to her. "Come over here." He picked her up and sat her on his lap, his hand on her knee. "Here's a waffle and some orange juice. I have some sad news."

"What's going on? Where's mother?"

"She's fine, but she had to leave. You know she had problems, and she's gone away to a home where she can rest and deal with her illness.

"Where? Can I go see her?"

"No, Rachel, she's in another state, in California."

"She didn't tell me anything. Why didn't I know?" She jumped down off his lap. "She wouldn't just leave like that. She wouldn't do that to me."

"We've been talking about it for a while, and we just heard about the opening at the home on Friday. We had to hurry. I'm sorry."

"What about me?"

"I've hired a woman to live here and to take care of you. Her name is Heather. She's coming over this afternoon to fix dinner and to get to know you."

Rachel glared at him. "I hate you. Leave me alone." She ran up the stairs, threw herself on her bed, and covered her head with pillows. She sobbed until she fell asleep.

She awoke to a knock on the door and then the door opening. A tall, slender woman with dark eyes and long brown hair walked over to the bedside. She had her hands on her hips, her head cocked, and a pinched face that looked like a cross between a smile and a frown. "I'm Heather. Your father hired me to take care of you."

Rachel pulled the covers over her face. "I don't want anyone to take care of me. Just go away."

"Sorry, not going to happen. Now do you want to get up and get dressed or should I drag your little ass out of there?" Heather grabbed the covers and threw them off. "We need to get off on the right foot. I'm the boss. You're the little girl. You do what I say, and we'll get along fine."

Rachel sat up and swung her feet off the bed. "I want to go find my mother. I don't like you."

Heather crossed her arms. "Like me or not—I could care less. But you will do as I say. Shall I pick out some clothes or do you want to get them yourself? You need to come downstairs and help me in the kitchen."

"I'll get dressed. Just get out of here and leave me alone."

"Okay, but if you're not downstairs in fifteen minutes, I'll be back."

"I've got homework. I'm not going to work in the kitchen."

"Your father said you need to learn to cook. You'll have to do the home-work later."

"My father said that?"

"That's right. He wants you to learn to cook and to be useful around the house. I guess your mother didn't teach you very well."

Rachel gathered up some clothes and ran into the bathroom. When she came into the kitchen, Heather had a cookbook on the table and was chopping some carrots and celery. She smelled like dish soap. "We're going to make a simple chicken casserole. Get that chicken out of the refrigerator, and I'll show you how to cut the meat off the bones."

When Rachel's father came home about seven, the table was set with the good china, the wine was on the table, and a hot casserole covered with light brown melted cheese and breadcrumbs was at the head of the table. Fresh flowers adorned the center.

He sat down, smiled, and poured Heather and himself some wine. Rachel drank water. "Now this is how a household should be. You pay attention Rachel. Heather is going to teach you how to be a useful wife someday."

After dinner, Rachel did the dishes and cleaned up the kitchen while she choked back tears. Heather had told her she could have one hour of TV, and then she needed to do her homework. Rachel marched to her room and shut the door. Later, after falling asleep, she heard noises and tip-toed down the stairs and peeked in her mother and father's bedroom. Heather was there with her father in bed. The nightlight shined on her slender, bare legs and arms. They were wrapped around her father, making shadows, and reminding Rachel of a huge, daddy-long-legs spider. Heather had moved in, just like that. Rachel grabbed the bedroom door handle, slammed the door shut, ran up the stairs, locked herself in the bathroom, and soaped and soaped herself in the shower. Her skin turned pink and squeaked when she rinsed, but she felt as though she was covered with scum and couldn't get clean.

"Rachel," her father shouted, banging on the door. "Turn off that shower. You're using up all the hot water."

She turned off the water and waited until he left before going to bed.

On several occasions, on her way out the door for school, Rachel met strange women coming out of Edward's bedroom. One Sunday morning, Rachel put a plate of waffles and sausage in front of Edward. "Does Heather know about the other women you bring home?"

"That's none of your concern. When Heather's not traveling, she's the only one."

"But you said you guys are engaged."

"Someday you'll learn. It's an open thing. Heather does what she wants, and I do what I want—makes for a better friendship." He wolfed down a waffle and two sausages. "Time to get this kitchen cleaned up."

Rachel wrinkled her nose and picked up his plate. "You're lucky you have a servant."

"If you live in this house, you'll earn your keep."

Rachel came and went as she pleased, hung out with friends at the mall, did her homework and kept the house clean. She kept out of trouble as far as Edward knew except for one costly incident when she was fifteen. Edward got a call at work in the middle of the day. "Mr. Curry, you'd better come to the Counselor's office right away."

"What? Who the hell is this?"

"I'm Jerome Buttrick, the principal at Rachel's school. You'd better come now."

"What's happening?"

"Two detectives are questioning Rachel. Something about forged checks. They're going to take her in."

"Tell them to hold on. I'm Rachel's attorney, and I'm on the way."

Rachel looked up as Edward blustered in the door. He pointed at Rachel "I'm Edward Curry, her father, and also her attorney. Now, what's this all about?"

One of the detectives stood up. "I'm detective Yonkers, and this is Detective Perry. He nodded but remained seated.

"Mr. Curry, we believe Rachel has written some bad checks at several women's clothing stores—about two-thousand dollars' worth."

"Are they overdrafts? We can cover them today."

"I'm afraid not. Rachel stole or found another student's checkbook—Linda Hampton—and forged her name. She also used Linda's school ID card."

Edward glared at Rachel. She hunched her shoulders, crossed her arms, and looked down at the floor.

"Mr. Curry, Rachel is a minor and you are her guardian, correct?"

"Yes, that's correct."

"May we have permission to search her backpack?"

Edward grabbed Rachel's bag and began dumping everything out on the table—books, notebooks, makeup, gym clothes, tampons, and a small wallet. He ripped open the wallet and found a blue checkbook for the bank account of Linda Hampton. He stared at Rachel with eyes of cold steel. She hunkered down even more in her chair. "I found the wallet. I didn't steal it."

"Don't say another word."

Edward turned to detective Yonkers. "Will you be taking her to juvenile detention."

"Yes, sir."

"If it is all the same to you, I'll take custody of her and bring her down-town myself. You can follow me if you'd like."

All right, Mr. Curry, we can accommodate that, but I need to take her backpack, her stuff, and that wallet."

In the car, Rachel began sobbing. "What's going to happen to me?"

"I should beat the living shit out of you. Do you realize how embarrassing this could be for my law firm?"

"Why would you care about anything I do?"

"I'm your father. People have expectations. Sometimes I don't know why I fought for your custody. You should have gone with your mother. It would have been good riddance to both of you."

"But then you wouldn't have a servant. That's all I am to you anyway." Rachel slumped over and held her face in her hands. She listened as Edward began making phone calls. "Listen, I need a favor," then "your honor, Edward Curry here. I've got a minor problem. I can take care of it before the day's out." Then he called his office and talked with his paralegal.

They pulled up to the juvenile detention center and walked into the reception area. The two detectives followed. Rachel was surprised to see two attorneys from Edward's office. They huddled for a moment, leaving Rachel in a straight-backed wooden chair.

A man appeared and walked up to the detectives. "Thanks for bringing her in. I'll take it from here." He stood Rachel up and handcuffed her hands behind her back. He pointed to the backpack. "Is that the evidence?"

"Yes, sir. Everything is in there."

"Okay, I've got it. Thank you for your smart work detectives." He led the way to an interrogation room, ushering Rachel by her elbow. Edward and the other two attorneys followed. Edward closed the door. "I appreciate this Richard—now I owe the prosecutor one."

"Teenagers. I've never figured out what to do with them. I think they lose their minds when they turn fourteen or fifteen."

One attorney whispered into Edward's ear. Edward shook his head and frowned. Rachel could see he was disgusted. Such an asshole.

The prosecutor unlocked Rachel's handcuffs. "The Hampton family has agreed not to press charges, and all four stores will let things go if they get reimbursed for all their costs."

Edward nodded. "Sounds good to me. I guess that's one less case for you to prosecute."

Richard pursed his lips and stared into Rachel's eyes. "Don't ever let me see you again young lady."

Rachel shook her head and offered a quivering smile. "Thank you."

Back in the car, Edward slammed his open palm across Rachel's face, her cheek reddening. Her ears rang, and blood dripped from her nose. "Five-thousand to the Hamptons and two-thousand to the stores. Except for school, I'm restricting you to the house for the next three months. I want that place to be spotless and meals ready on time. Do you understand?"

Rachel held a tissue to her nose. "Yes."

"Yes, what?"

"Yes, sir."

The following week Rachel's life changed. She found Heather's stash of valium in the nightstand drawer on her side of the bed. From that moment on, a gentle cloud covered Rachel's heart and soul. Rachel's fifteenth year and sixteenth birthday came and went. She lived in a peaceful fog and floated above the clamor and cares for her friends, teachers, and Heather and Edward. She kept her grades up and became a loner. When asked about her red eyes and slow reactions, she explained that she had allergies and had to take Benadryl. She managed her addiction carefully, and she never allowed herself to sink into despair.

Just before Thanksgiving after her sixteenth birthday, Edward had a stroke at his office while yelling at someone on the phone. Even after rehabilitation, he became paralyzed on his right side, and he lost his speech except for grunts and grumbles. Rachel had to take care of him because he lived in a wheelchair at home. Heather traveled more. She said that if Rachel were there, they would save money on home health care.

One morning while Rachel was wheeling Edward into the shower, she slipped and fell on the tile floor. She grabbed her knee with both hands. "Damn that hurts. I wish you would die."

Edward swung his left fist around, but it got tangled in the shower curtain as Rachel stood up and turned on the icy water. "Ughhh, ugh."

"Too bad it's cold, asshole. Wash the stink off yourself."

Just before Christmas break, the school Counselor called Rachel to her office. As she came in, she saw her mother Sandra dressed in a business suit and a white blouse. Her hair was cut to just below her ears, highlighting her face and her smile. She stood up. Rachel looked her up and down. "What the hell do you want?"

"I want to go for a walk and tell you some things."

"There's nothing I want to hear from you."

"You need to know the story."

"I don't give a shit. You left. That's the story."

"No, Rachel. There's a lot more."

"After eight years? Why now?"

"Because I heard about your father's stroke. He can't do anything to either one of us now."

Rachel tipped her head and looked at the Counselor. She nodded, and Rachel stood up, following Sandra out the door and then out past the football field. Sandra chose her words. "I know you're angry. I know you think I abandoned you, and in a way, I did. But we are both alive, and that's something."

Rachel clenched her fists. "Why did you leave me? I was just a little kid."

"He beat me nearly to death and took me to the emergency room. He told everyone I had been mugged, raped, and beaten by a man in a parking garage. He even took me there and rolled me around on the concrete—you know, made a fake crime scene. He said if I didn't disappear, he would kill both you and me."

"What happened? Why did he beat up on you?"

"One night I saw him going into your room in his bathrobe. You had just turned eight. I followed him. He lifted your covers and touched you. He didn't know I was there. I hit him on the back with a baseball bat—told him I would go to the police if he hurt you. He got dressed, said he was sorry and left the house. I fell asleep on the couch, and when I woke up, he was standing over me and stuck a needle into my thigh. The next thing I remember was the concrete floor of the parking garage and the smell of tires, gasoline, and my blood. He wore leather gloves and beat me for a long time. I woke up in the emergency room listening to him whispering in my ear. "You need to disappear. If you say anything at all, I'll kill both of you.""

Rachel took a breath. "Where have you been?"

"After I healed up some in the hospital, I took the five thousand dollars he gave me and moved to Los Angeles. I got a job with an insurance agency, and I've been there ever since."

Rachel sat down on the grass. "I needed you, don't you know that? You could've called or something."

Sandra sat down beside her and held her hand. "I couldn't take the chance. I love you so much. It broke my heart." Sandra hugged Rachel.

"Can I come live with you now?"

. "Legally your father has custody until you're eighteen, but given his condition, I think we can petition the court. I'll work on getting a job in Albuquerque. Edward can't do anything now. I wish that stroke had killed him."

"Yeah, me too."

"I've got a question."

"What's that?"

"What are we going to do about you?"

"About me?"

"You're high on something. Oxy?"

"I take valium now and then for anxiety. Sometimes Librium."

"From a doctor?"

Rachel dropped her head. "No, I take them from Heather, Edward's girlfriend—she never misses them."

Sandra pulled Rachel near her and stroked her hair. "We'll be okay now. It will take some time, but we'll get through this."

"Maybe you'll be okay, but I've got to take care of that bastard." Rachel stood up. "I'd better get back to class. Please leave me alone. This is a lot to handle."

"Sure. I understand." Sandra dug into her purse. "Here's a cell phone. It's for you, and my number is in your Contacts under Mom."

Rachel's life settled into the humdrum beat of a routine: attend Edward in the morning, greet the part-time home care worker, go to school, come back, relieve the home care worker, prepare Edward's dinner, bourbon cocktails for Edward with a straw, homework, Edward's nasty bathroom business, and roll Edward into bed. On the weekends Heather came home and wrote herself checks for Edward to sign with his working hand. Sometimes she would stay in his bedroom. In the mornings, she frowned, muttered, and took long showers. "See you next week. I've got meetings in Chicago. Take care of our man."

"Yeah, sure." Rachel had pocketed another three week's supply from Heather's purse, and always kept a perpetual stash that would last six months. Sandra called every two weeks or so, and although Rachel was civil, she didn't want to talk with her. The custody issue got jammed up with the courts since Sandra had to pay the attorney in installments. "We're making progress, but it's slow. Edward's partners keep putting up roadblocks."

"This will never happen before I'm eighteen," Rachel said. "Then it won't matter."

The day after her seventeenth birthday on a Saturday, Rachel fed Edward his breakfast and wheeled him out on the back porch, parked him by the edge, and put a blanket on his lap.

"Edward, I can't stand your sour smell and your stupid grunts and shouts. You're a poor excuse for a human being. Have a beautiful day."

Rachel took the car, went to the store, stopped at the gym to buy a membership, and then drove around until after four. Did she remember to set the brake on the wheelchair? When she got home, Heather's car was there along with an ambulance. Heather ran out the door waving her arms. "Where have you been? Edward tumbled off the porch. This mess is your fault."

"Is he hurt?"

"He's dead, Rachel, he's dead. The paramedics said he broke his neck. Where were you?"

"At the store, getting his dinner."

"Why did you leave him on the porch?"

"The weather's nice. Edward wanted some fresh air. He smelled bad."

Heather put her hands on her hips and glared. "You know you're not my kid. Don't expect me to take care of you."

"I know. I'll take care of myself."

"You can stay here until you're eighteen. Then I'm selling the house."

"No, I'll leave right away. This place makes me sick. My mother's in Albuquerque. I'll call her and tell her the news—she'll be brokenhearted."

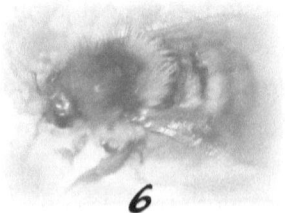

6

⊙n a bright, sunny day in May in 2005, Michelle Peterson walked into Dr. Jeff Corley's office. She put her hands and purse on the reception counter.

"My name is Michelle Peterson, and I've got broken a tooth. I met Jeff, I mean, Dr. Corley last year and he said to stop in if he could ever be of help. Is there any chance he's available?"

Rachel, Jeff's receptionist and hygienist looked up. "You mean without an appointment?"

"Yes. We became friends, and he said I could stop by anytime."

Rachel stood up. "Let me check."

She walked back to Jeff's lab. "There's a Michelle Peterson here. She has a broken tooth, and she said you told her she could stop in anytime."

"Is her right eyebrow higher than her left one?"

"Yeah, she looks like she's a judge or something. You should watch out. I think she's on the prowl."

"Give me ten minutes."

Rachel threw a curled smile at Michelle. "He'll be with you in a few minutes."

Michelle sat down in a nearby waiting room chair and looked around. His waiting room featured a long tall aquarium teeming with salt water fish. Orange clown fish and blue angel fish swam among branches of pink coral, and little yellow seahorses bounced off the bottom. Silver framed and matted modern art and landscapes hung on two walls like a gallery. Overstuffed tan leather furniture and mahogany side tables covered with expensive magazines and plastic plants completed the picture. Hung on the hallway wall leading to the dental rooms there were two dozen framed certificates, degrees, awards, licenses, continuing education certificates, and photographs of people with bright dental smiles. To the untrained eye, his office appeared well-appointed and elegant. As the sun set in the evenings, however, the air reeked of what it was—jumbled pretense. Everything was rented and came from different vendors. To a designer's eye, it all appeared expensive, but nothing quite fit together, like pieces in a furniture store tent sale.

At quiet times, when Rachel looked critically, she became troubled. Jeff paid eight-hundred dollars a month for furniture, four-hundred for art, and three-hundred for the aquarium maintenance agreement with a local pet store. He also paid a leasing company eighteen-hundred a month for dental equipment, and his landlord appeared early on the first of the month and collected fifteen-hundred for rent. Not counting Rachel's salary and cleaning, Jeff needed five-thousand a month for his fixed costs, a tall order for a solo practice. The casinos had become the source of his second income, sometimes. Credit cards filled the gaps.

Jeff came out into the waiting room.

"Hi Michelle," he said, giving her a gentle side hug. "What's going on? You're back in town. Are you doing okay?"

"My marriage ended after two months, and I've been working as an ER nurse in a hospital in Portland. It rains all the time, and I need the sunshine. So, I'm looking for a job in Albuquerque—I have a couple of interviews. But I broke a tooth sometime in the night."

"Come in. Let's look."

Rachel helped Michelle into a chair and put a drape on her chest.

"Open. It's the first bicuspid, upper right. You broke off the top half. Did you bite down on something? Hard candy?"

"No, I woke up and felt it with my tongue."

"It looks like it was decayed. Does it hurt?"

"It aches a little, but it doesn't hurt."

"You're going to need a crown, so I need to take an impression. I need to get this tooth ready first. You'll feel a little sting." He injected a little Novocain and prepared the tooth. After he had taken the impression, Jeff got his color chart from his lab. He held it up to her front teeth. "Rachel, look. Does this color match?"

"Yes, that's the one."

"Are you sure? I want perfection."

"That's the color, Dr. Corley. I'm sure of it."

Jeff made a temporary crown in his lab while Michelle waited. "Take a little nap. This won't take long."

He put the temporary crown on Michelle's tooth. "Now bite down on this gauze roll for a few minutes. Are you doing okay?"

"Uh, huh."

Jeff stepped into his lab and then returned. He took the gauze roll from her mouth and leaned in close to her. Michelle looked up. "Your cologne intrigues me—you smell spicy. Oh, am I being too personal?"

Jeff touched his cheek to her nose. "There's supposed to be a hint of melon, eucalyptus, and mango. Can you smell it? —Called Escape by Calvin Klein. It's my daytime cologne. Expensive."

Michelle raised her nose, sniffing. "You wear it well."

"I'm glad you like it." He touched the tooth with his mirror. "I love crowns. They're my favorite because I get to change weakness into strength. Know what I mean? Plus, I can make sure your right bicuspid is as strong as your left one. He smiled with a twinkle in his eye. "I'll make them even so they match perfectly."

Michelle frowned. "I have no idea what you're talking about. How much is this going to cost me?"

Jeff glanced down at Michelle's cleavage. Her lavender smell drew the rest of his attention. "I told you I would help you out, so this one is on the house. The crown should be ready Friday morning. That's my day off. Why don't you come in about 9 am and then we'll go to breakfast and get caught up?"

Michelle got up from the chair. "Now that's what I call customer service. Thank you. I'll see you then."

Rachel walked her to the door. Michelle paused in the hallway. "Who is the smiling woman in that photo?"

"Oh, that's Jeff's mother, Mom. He's very proud of his work. With that new smile, her face came alive."

"He worked on his mother?"

"It was one of his first restorations. Mom was delighted."

"Was?"

"Yes. She died of cancer several years ago."

"Oh, I'm sorry to hear that."

"He doesn't like to talk about it."

"Okay, I understand."

Rachel touched her arm. "Dr. Corley will expect you a little before nine in the morning on Friday. Please don't be late. You're lucky. He doesn't come in on his day off."

"I'll be here."

Rachel marched into Jeff's lab. "Well, here you go again. You need to watch yourself, Jeff Corley. This girl's a strong one. She'll toss you for a loop."

"No, I don't think so."

"There's something about her that bothers me, something you won't like."

"Well, thank you for your concern, but I think I can handle myself. What's the matter? Are you jealous?"

"Oh, come on, we got over that long ago."

Jeff thought back to when they first met. He had interviewed Rachel for a job as a receptionist and hygienist three years before. She was an R.N., and on her second leave from work as part of a diversion program.

"I have to be honest," she said. "I have a problem with morphine, and my program works well when I'm away from my job at the hospital. There's something about the environment. I want to try something new. I was a hygienist before I got my R.N. degree, and I have excellent people skills. Could you give me a chance?"

There was something about her bold honesty, her red hair, and the feisty look in her eye that charmed Jeff. He rubbed his chin. To him, at that moment, she appeared to be an energetic little six-year-old girl who wanted to play, and a grown voluptuous woman in search of someone, all rolled into one. For some reason, he could not resist. Perhaps there was still the hint of compassion in his heart.

"Sure, I'll give you a chance. We'll try it for ninety days, and if you stay clean and if you're good at what you do, we'll see about a more permanent position."

Rachel did an excellent job. After three months, Jeff extended benefits, including health insurance, and began taking Rachel for lunch. Their friendship grew, and one weekend he talked her into coming home with him to see what else their friendship had to offer. Their sex was tepid and awkward.

"What's the problem? Don't I turn you on?"

"It isn't you, Jeff. You are a remarkable man, all that any woman could ask for, but I prefer women. I thought maybe with you I would be different. Please don't take this personally."

Jeff dressed and picked up his car keys. "I knew it was you. Let's go."

He drove her home in silence, both hands gripping the steering wheel. She was crying when she got out of the car. "Do I still have a job?"

Jeff was dumbfounded. He had always thought his sexual prowess would be more than enough for anyone. He thought he could arouse the deepest desire with any woman, the evolutionary urge to procreate—even with a lesbian. Pissed him off.

Rachel sensed danger in the air and asked again. "Do I still have a job?"

He took a breath, bit his lip, and looked straight ahead. "Yes."

That weekend Rachel relapsed and didn't show up for work on Monday. At noon, Jeff went to her apartment and found her unconscious in bed. He called for an ambulance and waited until the paramedic put her on a gurney. "She's breathing, but we need to transport. We'll take her to Presbyterian downtown. Does she have family we can call?"

"No, I'm her employer, and I have her medical power of attorney."

"Guess she's been through this before, huh?"

Jeff looked around the apartment, found Rachel's stash in the medicine cabinet, and threw it out. Then, for some reason he did not understand, Jeff shepherded Rachel through a thirty-day rehab program in Santa Fe. He hired temporary help in the meantime, and then he invited her back to work on a drug contract. Rachel often told Jeff that he must be some weird angel sent by God himself, and her gratitude melted into her role as a loving helpmate and best friend. On that day of her relapse, there must have been a tiny fissure in Jeff's soul, and Rachel slipped in. Yes, they were past that, and Jeff had done dental work for a couple of Rachel's girlfriends. They had praised his near-perfect work and helped him develop a niche market of cosmetic dentistry for the gay and lesbian community in Albuquerque.

Jeff felt confused when Rachel had told him about her family. Her mother had died of an overdose soon after reappearing in her life to claim her. Now, she had no one. He didn't know what to do when she asked him to be her medical power of attorney, so he agreed. Even after talking with Ben about Rachel and her history, Jeff could not fathom how she could be a little girl and a grown woman at the same time. Ben said it was how Jeff saw her, not how she truly was. It had to do with her brokenness and the hint of compassion that was buried deep in Jeff's heart. Ben was hopeless. That didn't make any sense at all. Ben said Jeff's behavior reminded him of a worker bee taking care of the queen.

Jeff smiled at Rachel, nodding his head. "Yes, I know better than that. You're a good friend who prefers women."

Jeff was competent, but he was glad he had someone to watch out for him. Today he had that look in his eye, a shifty glimmer that meant his anxiety was getting out of control. "Rachel, could you stay late or come back after dinner?"

"I could come back later if you need me."

"It's time for my treatment. The gerbils are running loose in my head again."

Rachel was the only woman Jeff trusted. He relied on her to handle all his billing, his money, scheduling, patients, and tonight as a companion who watched over him while he entered an anxiety-reducing bubble with nitrous oxide. Nitro was his drug of choice—essentially harmless—but he had mild worries about nausea and aspirating, dizziness, and depersonalization that would let him float above his body and watch himself as though he was a robot on TV. Usually, he was all right, but since the time he had gotten up out of the dental chair, fallen, and hurt his hand, he was more comfortable if Rachel was there. She would sit and read while he inhaled Nitronox mixed with oxygen. She would steady him when he got up, and he loved her smell, bright sweet lemongrass. It brought him down to earth and made him feel clean. She would drive him home if he felt like he couldn't drive. Although annoying, Rachel also offered her opinions about all the women that Jeff dated and tried to wave him off from the gold-diggers, even though there was little gold to dig and his credit cards were maxed out. She often had to wait to cash her paycheck.

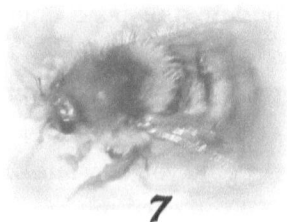

7

*M*ichelle came to Jeff's office at nine sharp on Friday morning, and he got to work. He fit her crown a couple of times until it was just right, and then cemented it in place.

"Here, bite down on this gauze roll for a few minutes."

He cleaned tiny dabs of cement from her gum line and then gave her a hand mirror.

"Jeff, this is perfect. I can't even tell it's a crown."

"All in a day's work. As I said, I love crowns. Rachel was right. The color is a perfect match."

"Are you sure I can't pay you something, at least for your time?"

"Yes, I'm sure. Come on, I'll take you to Flying Star, and you can buy our coffee. We can split a cinnamon roll. Leave your car here, and we'll take my Beemer."

They found a quiet table toward the back.

"I know it has been a while since you've been to Albuquerque. Did your ex-husband take you on the Tram?"

"No, he said it made him dizzy."

"Well, my apartment is north on Academy, out by the Tram. We could go up the mountain and walk around some, maybe have a light lunch, and I could show you my place. How does that sound?"

Michelle put her finger on her upper lip. "Sure, I didn't have any plans except for this crown. Is it cold on the crest? I didn't bring a jacket."

"No problem. I've got an extra jacket in the car. We'll be fine."

They finished their coffee and drove to the base of the Tram. When he tried to get tickets, Visa declined Jeff's credit card. He walked over to Michelle. "I forgot my credit card and didn't have much cash. Can I put these tickets on your card and pay you back?"

"Of course."

They stepped into a tram car just before a scheduled departure. They were the only passengers for this ride up and had the car to themselves.

"Looks like the lunch crowd is already up top, and tourist season hasn't ramped up yet. Wow, we're all alone. Check out that view."

Michelle stood at one corner looking to the south and west. She crossed her hands over her chest. "This is exciting Jeff. I've never seen anything like it."

Jeff came up behind her and put one hand on each railing at her sides. She was trapped, but his body was only a light touch on her back. "I feel great up here. Albuquerque is my town, Michelle. As far as you can see, this is my city."

Michelle squirmed around until her face was close to his, almost touching. Jeff kissed her with a gentle and lingering kiss. Michelle reached down and loosened one of his arms from the railing. "That was fun, Jeff, but I feel trapped."

He moved aside. "Sorry. I just felt like being close to you. And we're alone. And this ride is exhilarating. And you're quite beautiful, you know. Your ex-husband is an idiot. He should have taken better care of you. I'll bet you didn't know that I've thought of you often since we met last year. I've wondered what happened."

"Well, now you know, and I have a new crown, and we're on a Tram car, and I'm looking for a job in Albuquerque, and you just kissed me. That about covers it except for this beautiful suede jacket and the breath mints in the pocket. The lining feels like silk."

"You should try it with your shirt off. It feels way sensual."

"Well, maybe we should save that for another time. We're almost to the top."

They walked around on the Crest for an hour or so, had a light lunch, and then caught another car down. This time it was crowded, so they stood on the side. She leaned back against Jeff, and he put his hands around her waist.

It was just a few minutes to Jeff's apartment. He had a three-bedroom at the Pavilions and a balcony deck that captured an unobstructed view of the mountains.

He ushered Michelle into the living room.

"Wow. Your place is beautiful. Do you have a roommate?"

"Only Budgey over there." He pointed to a cage on a stand with a little blue parakeet hopping from perch to perch. "Otherwise it's mine alone. I like to have extra room for guests if necessary."

Michelle walked over and cooed at Budgey and then wandered into the kitchen gleaming with all stainless-steel appliances and ivory-colored Corian countertops. The cabinets were a light pecan.

"This kitchen is gorgeous. Do you cook?"

"Not often, but when I do it's a masterpiece—everything I need is here." He opened cabinets to show her food processors, juicers, blenders, an array of glass bowls, and an elaborate set of Williams-Sonoma all clad copper cookware.

"Once I prepared a six-course meal for eight. It took all day, but everyone loved it."

The living room featured a large print, a Wilson Hurley landscape over six feet long.

"That painting is beautiful, majestic."

"One of my favorites. That's Wilson Hurley's *The Sandias from Algodones*, from two thousand seven. It's a signed print. I picked it up after I moved in, and it seems perfect for that wall, don't you think?"

"Yes. And you can step out on the balcony and see the real Sandias. Oh, Jeff, thank you so much for taking me up on the Tram."

Jeff made cups of hot Chai tea. "Would you like sugar?"

"No, just plain is fine."

She walked around the apartment looking at his books, furniture, pleated window shades, and monogrammed towels. "This bathroom is luxurious."

"Check out the one in the master bedroom."

Michelle held her cup in both hands and stepped into the master bedroom. "My gosh, Jeff, where did you get that painting?"

Jeff had acquired Steve Hank's *Sheer Grace*, and it was featured on the wall first visible when entering the bedroom, the wall opposite a fluffy white, down comforter, spread out on a king-size bed.

"It's called *Sheer Grace*. It's a signed limited edition. Beautiful, don't you think?"

"Oh, my gosh, look at these. These paintings are all nudes. Same artist, right?"

"Yes, Steve Hanks, all signed, all limited editions. That one's called *Wonders of a Woman*, and under that is *Like and Angel*. The two smaller ones on the sides are *Interior View* and *Time Standing Still*."

Michelle put her hand up to her mouth. "They're exquisite, but I'm feeling self-conscious. These women seem perfect. I've never seen watercolors like these. Have you seen real women who look like this?"

"He uses live models. He might take some liberties with how he paints what he sees, but they're real women. Check out the bathroom."

Michelle wandered into the master bath. The turquoise tiled shower was enclosed with glass, and the jacuzzi bathtub was oversized.

"This is beautiful. I am impressed. You have a gorgeous apartment. Your dental practice must be lucrative."

"Thanks. Yes, I've been successful. Excuse me. I'm going to take a shower."

"A shower now?"

"The ride on the Tram was dusty. I like to stay fresh and clean."

Michelle was on the couch reading a magazine as he came out into the living room with a large bath towel wrapped around his waist. She raised both eyebrows as he rubbed skin lotion on his muscled arms, chest, and stomach. "Shouldn't you be doing that in the bathroom?"

"No, I'm comfortable right here. I need a little more tea. After that ride up the mountain and all that walking, I bet you'd feel better if you took a shower. There's a new terry cloth robe hanging on the back of the door."

Michelle crossed her arms. "So, is this the moment?"

"The moment?"

"Yes, the moment when we decide to have sex?"

"I thought maybe we should take a nap." He grinned. "I don't have the TV on, and I don't like to watch *Law and Order*." He struck a pose like a bodybuilder. "I guess that's a start."

Michelle put her head down, perhaps hiding a smile, and walked into the bathroom. Soon Jeff heard the water running.

When she came out wrapped in his robe, Jeff was naked on his side on top of the comforter. Flickers of sunlight rippled over his shoulders and chest. He was smiling.

"My gosh, Jeff, have you no shame?" She said this, but she thought, *now this is what drop- dead-gorgeous means.*

He smiled. "Well, Michelle, sometimes people like to look at me. I want to be obliging."

"I can't believe you said that. I don't know if I like this."

"Come over here and let's find out."

Melissa sat down beside him. He nuzzled her neck, slipping the robe off her shoulders.

"Jeff, did you change your cologne?"

"You noticed. Supposed to have an oriental scent, exotic, saffron wood."

She leaned back. "I smell vanilla and nutmeg, too. What's it called?"

"Noir Extreme. Supposed to be mysterious."

Jeff was gentle, practiced, and thorough. Michelle yielded to all his ways and cried out a couple of times. After a while, Jeff snuggled next to her and ever-so-gently moved his arm, so it pushed her left breast up level with her right one. "You know I love your lavender smell. It suits you."

"Hey, what are you doing?"

"Humor me. I'm just evening things out."

Michelle sat up, covering herself with the comforter.

"This is not funny, Jeff. We've been over this before." She took his hand and placed it on her breast under the comforter. "You can touch but not lift—rearranging me is off limits. Understand?"

"Okay—for now."

"Please try to understand. When you do that, I feel objectified, like a mannequin, not like a woman making love. You are an incredible lover, Dr. Corley, but it all goes away when you rearrange me. I like you a lot. It seems like there is something here, but if you do that, then we can't do this."

"Don't be upset with me. You're an exciting woman. You may be the woman I need, and I don't want to mess it up. Come on, let's get some clothes on and I'll make you a cheese omelet. You like omelets?"

"Sure. After that workout, I'm famished."

After they ate and watched *Million Dollar Baby* on his widescreen, Jeff took her back to her car at the office. He opened the door for her, and after she had got in, he leaned down and kissed her. It was a long kiss, probing with his tongue. She jerked away with a loud slurp. What are you doing? Are you feeling my crown with your tongue?"

"I was just checking the margins—wanted to make sure they were perfect."

"Well, I can come in, sit in a chair, and you can check with your light. For God's sake, don't check with your tongue when you're kissing me. What's with you, Jeff?"

"I wanted my work to be perfect and for you to look good. That's all. Would you like to be with me next Friday?"

"Yes, I would, Jeff. With a few exceptions, today has been glorious."

"Okay, let's meet here about noon."

"See you then."

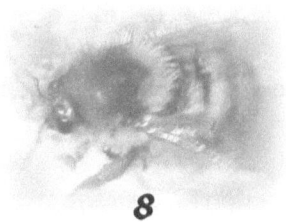

8

*J*eff and Michelle met every weekend for a month. They settled into a routine of movies, eating out, walks in the park, time at the Nature Center, and passionate nights. In a visit to Ben's office, Jeff told Ben things with Michelle looked hopeful.

"She has those little deformities, but everything else seems right."

"She's the one with the raised eyebrow, right? You told me about her."

"Yes, and her right breast is higher than her left one, and her smile lifts the right side of her face more than the left. Everything else is good except sometimes her mind is all over the place. Remember? You said she might have an attention deficit disorder."

"Easily distracted?"

"Yes, but she sure can focus if she wants to. Her attention to my body is lavish—I've got her trained to know what I like. Michelle likes to please me."

"Well, lucky you. That takes care of your rule number one—you are your body, right?"

"You're getting to know me. Thanks for not judging."

Ben smiled. "Oh, I judge you all right, and I even diagnose you. I just don't tell you about it. I think I'd rather just be your friend. You remind me of my drones in the hive. They're lazy, can't take care of their own needs, and have only one purpose."

"One purpose? What's that?"

"To breed with the queen. They fly two or three hundred feet in the air and gather around a virgin queen. It's a dangerous lovefest. Of course, Michelle is no virgin, but still, you pursue her and expect her to meet your needs. But you'd better be careful."

"Why's that?"

"The drone's sex organ is barbed and stays in there. After mating, a drone's sex organ and a major part of the internal anatomy tear away, and each drone falls to its death."

"Well I'm not lazy, and Michelle's not a virgin, so your drone analogy doesn't fit."

"Arise to the metaphor, my friend. Don't define yourself with your body and your sex organ. It could lead to death. You have more than one purpose. Don't hear me judging you because I'm not."

"That's good because I don't trust anyone else. Besides, you do a lot of guessing, and I don't say anything unless I'm right. I like to go with what I know."

Ben shook his head. "You do believe that, don't you? You're a classic, Jeff."

"Like an elegant classic Mercedez Benz?"

"No, like a classic narcissistic personality disorder. If there were a king bee, you'd be him."

"Well, if I have to be classic, the narcissist is a good choice. At least I get what I want and what I deserve. Getting what I want is not a disorder."

"See. That's classic, right out of the DSM-IV."

"Just be grateful I helped you with your dissertation without charging you anything. Most subjects get paid. Hey, maybe I'll bring Michelle by to meet you."

"It would be better in a social context. Keep your eye open for an opportunity."

Near the end of June, Michelle called Jeff's office.

"Hi, Rachel. Please ask Jeff to call me. I have some good news."

"He's not with anyone. Hold a minute."

"Hi, Michelle. What's up?"

"I got a job."

"Where, at Presbyterian?"

"No, at a Family Practice nearby. It's over on Eubank, and they have four doctors. They need an RN to manage the Medical Assistants and supervise the state vaccine program. I'm sure I'll do other things, too. I start Monday."

"Hey, congratulations. That'll keep you busy and out of my hair."

"You just think so. That's not going to happen. There's one thing, though. I may have to work some Saturdays."

"What about me?"

"You may be alone some Saturdays, but not often. And guess what? They are having a fourth of July picnic, and they invited me. It's on Sunday for everyone's convenience. I'm supposed to bring a friend. Are you up for that?"

"I guess, but I won't stay long. Standing around with a crowd of people bores me."

The picnic was at one of the doctors' houses on Canada del Oso in High Desert. Garcia Tents installed large canopies in the backyard, and the main serving table featured an array of catered food. Easy listening music played from speakers in the background, and two bartenders were mixing drinks and setting out beer and soft drinks. The house was pueblo style and opened to views of the Sandia Mountains, a beautiful setting. The tramway was visible to the south.

"Hello Dr. Douglas," Michelle said. "This is my friend Dr. Corley. He's a cosmetic dentist, and his office is not far from the Medical Clinic—he's on Osuna."

"Please call me Jeff."

"Hello, Jeff. I'm Jeremy."

"You have a beautiful home. Thank you for the invitation."

"Come meet my partners."

They stepped under a bright red and white canopy near the back fence.

"Dr. Jeff Corley, I'd like for you to meet John Dunlevy, Enrico Morales, and Leonard Goldstein, my partners. Michelle, you've already met everyone, and we are all eager for you to start work. We need the help."

"Thank you. I'm ready for a new challenge."

Jeff put on his best smile and greeted everyone. Each of the wives introduced themselves, and everyone made their way to the bar for drinks. Jeff stayed with iced tea. He didn't want to take a chance on being out of control. Sometimes alcohol loosened him up too much.

Jeff and Jeremy stepped toward the back wall, and adobe wall about four feet high.

"This view is outstanding," Jeff said. "Reminds me of my apartment. I live down the street at the Pavillions. I have a unit on the second floor that has a balcony that captures this same view. I plan on having a home built here in High Desert."

"Great. Maybe we'll be neighbors. You'd better pick out a lot soon. They're selling fast, and the price keeps going up."

Michelle walked up with Jeremy's wife, Margaret.

"Margaret wants to show us something, Jeff," Michelle said.

Margaret pointed to the right, toward the south. "This is open space on the other side of the wall, but our neighbors were happy to let us put a couple of beehives out there. There are so many flowers for the bees to choose. It's a perfect spot. The bees range up to the mountain."

"Those white boxes?" Michelle asked.

"We have two hives. They're a lot of work, but our sons enjoy helping me with them. It has become an enjoyable hobby. See how those worker bees come and go? It's amazing. There are probably 50,000 bees in each hive. We'll harvest honey soon."

Michelle walked closer. "That's fascinating. You have one queen bee in each hive, right?"

"Yes, and each one can produce 1,500 eggs per day. That's more than their body weight. Queens can't feed or groom themselves, and they can't leave the hive to relieve themselves. So, the worker bees feed them, care for them, and keep their surroundings clean."

Michelle smiled. "She really is a queen—royalty, raised in luxury."

"Yes. The best ones are gentle and productive, often for three years."

"Does it get too hot here in the sun?"

"Believe it or not, the worker bees fan their wings to regulate the temperature."

Jeff took several steps back and moved in behind Michelle. She turned. "What is it, Jeff?"

"I don't do well with bees," he whispered. He stepped back further.

"What do you mean?"

"Remember? I told you I hate bees, and they hate me."

"Why?"

"Does it matter? Let's walk over here under the tent."

"But I don't understand."

Out of nowhere, a sentry bee landed on Jeff's upper lip and stung him. Then another one stung him on the neck. Jeff turned and ran to the other end of the yard, under the portal on the house, scooped up a handful of ice and put the ice on his lip. Michelle followed. "Sonovabitch, this hurts." He sat down, hands shaking. John followed them. "Let me see. Jeff, your lips are swelling. Are you breathing okay?"

"Yes, I, fine."

"Are you allergic to bee stings?"

"I'm not allergic. They hate me. I've been stung before—lots of times, as a kid."

Jeremy hurried into the house and came back out with an EpiPen.

"I don't need that. I said I'm not allergic."

"Your lips are swelling. Sit still, Jeff." He stuck Jeff in the shoulder. "Let's use an abundance of caution. Gosh, I'm sorry. The bees have never come over the wall before."

"I'm a target for bees," Jeff said. "Just like when I was little. They're a menace."

"Just rest for a little while. I'll come back and check on you."

Jeff stood up and turned to Michelle. "Come on, let's go."

"Now?"

"Yes, now." He grabbed Michelle's arm, marched to the car, and drove away.

"You shouldn't have brought me here. I've told you I hate bees. They always sting me."

"I didn't know Margaret kept bee hives."

"You should've checked before you invited me." Jeff slammed his hand on the steering wheel.

"I had no idea, Jeff. It didn't occur to me."

"Well, it should have."

"Drop me off at my car, Jeff. I don't want to argue. I need to go back. I'll make up something about you resting."

"Tell them I had work in my lab. Don't say anything else. Understand?"

"Yes, I'll tell them you're polishing crowns or something."

"Dammit, just say I'm working in my lab. Don't get cute with me."

Jeff pulled into his office parking lot next to Michelle's car and got out.

Jeff poked his finger at Michelle. "You need to think about what you've done. I need your respect."

Michelle started crying. "Should I call you?"

"No, I'll call when I'm ready."

Michelle shook her head, got in her car, and drove away. Jeff got back in his BMW and headed to Santa Ana Casino in Bernalillo. He hadn't tried their blackjack tables for a while. He needed some good luck.

Jeff got a five-hundred dollar advance on a spare credit card he kept in the car. He drank, ate lobster at the buffet, and circulated among blackjack tables all night. When he left about dawn, he had two-hundred dollars in his pocket. He went home, took a shower, and went to his office.

Sister Mary Catherine brought two six-year-old boys to see Jeff. They sat in the waiting room, heads down.

"Dr. Corley, these little tykes need dental work and their moms can't afford it."

Jeff smiled. "No problem, Sister. I'll take care of these guys. Hey, boys, don't worry. I won't hurt you."

Rachel helped the first little boy, Rusty, into the chair and put a Nitronox mask on him. "Pretend this is a space-cadet mask. You'll soon be in outer space."

He looked wary, but he smiled at her. Jeff waited a few minutes and then injected Novocain around the decayed teeth. He pulled four rotten baby teeth, and put fillings in five permanent teeth. He was quick, and Rusty felt no pain.

Rachel helped Rusty out of the chair. "Rusty, I think you're space travel is over, and it's time to land."

He blinked and laughed. Rachel helped him walk into the waiting room, and he fell into Sister Mary Catherine's ample lap.

"Are you feeling okay, Rusty?"

He shook his head up and down. "I'm a space cadet."

"And who is this young man?" Rachel asked.

"I'm Eddie."

"Come with me, and you can be a space cadet too."

Eddies' teeth needed lots of work. Jeff spent an hour filling cavities and pulling two teeth that had grown in sideways. He took off his gloves and nodded at Rachel. She put his mask back on for a couple of minutes.

"That's enough," Jeff said. He put on fresh gloves. "These extractions are terrible."

He nodded once again at Rachel. She helped Eddie from the chair. "Hey, little man. Ready to land?"

She walked Eddie back into the waiting room, and Sister hugged him. In the meantime, Michelle had stomped into the waiting room and sat down, folded hands in her lap. She looked over at Sister. "What's going on with these little guys?" she asked.

"I'm Sister Mary Catherine, and I bring little kids to see Dr. Corley every couple of weeks. Their parents can't afford dental work, so Dr. Corley contributes his time. He is a saint. Don't know what I'd do without him."

Rachel looked at Michelle. "Do you need to see Jeff?"

Michelle stood up, took a deep breath, shook her head, and walked to the door. "I did need to see him, but it can wait. Don't tell him I was here, okay?"

"Okay, I'll see you later."

Jeff went home early, ran on the treadmill in the Pavillions gym, showered and climbed into bed at eight. He was exhausted. At eleven he woke up in a cold sweat. Emmy Lou's huge eye had appeared in a dream, along with his unreachable old well house floating in the sky, a pulsing view of the back of his father's head, and the smell of diesel fuel. He shook his head and sniffed his hands. The diesel smell followed him into his awakened state. He got up and sprayed body spray on his hands—Obsession by Calvin Klein. He started a pot of coffee and wandered around his apartment talking to Budgey who obliged him by chirping and hopping. His lip still hurt from the bee sting.

"What's wrong with me, Budgey? I can't sleep a whole night through. What's happening? Why don't people respect me?"

Jeff went out on the balcony, drank coffee, and stared at the dark mountains as his mind raced through options: *move away, marry Michelle, find a new woman, go to a new casino, do some cocaine, try sex again with Rachel.* No thought formed. He could hold only floating pieces. He smelled lavender, lemongrass, and his underarm perspiration. He felt trapped, boxed in by his jumbled mind. He needed something.

Just before dawn, he fell asleep on the couch for a couple of hours. At seven he called Michelle.

9

"*H*i, Michelle. Getting ready for work?"

"Hello, Jeff. Yes. How have you been? Are your bee stings better?"

"They're gone."

"That's good. What's on your mind at seven in the morning on a sunny day?"

"I'm cooking for a couple of people Saturday night, Chicken Cordon Blue, new potatoes, snow peas, and cinnamon ice cream from The Range for dessert. Would you like to come for dinner?"

"I work until five. Would six be too late?"

"No, six is just right."

"Do I know the couple?"

"I'd say so. You've seen them naked in the afternoon sunlight."

"Jeff..."

"Yes, just us. I need you, Michelle."

"Is it a formal dinner? What should I wear?"

"How about your purple thong?"

Michelle chuckled. "I'll see you about six on Saturday. I'll pick up a bottle of Chardonnay."

Jeff had the table set with candles and white China. When Michelle arrived she was fresh and vibrant, as though something important lay ahead. Jeff greeted her with a warm hug and a lingering kiss on her neck.

"Let's sit down. Dinner is ready."

He opened the wine and poured their glasses full. Motown music played in the background.

"I love Marvin Gaye," Michelle said. "I didn't know you listened to Motown. You've never played this music before—at least when I'm here."

"Yes, my secret is out. I like Lionel Richie and Smokey Robinson, but Marvin Gaye is the best. Helps me feel alive."

"Michael Jackson?"

"Not so much."

"Wait, so Marvin Gaye is your favorite, and your favorite song is *Let's Get It On*? Just guessing."

"I like *How Sweet It Is To Be Loved By You*. Always have. Both songs are coming up soon on the playlist. Let's eat. I want to know your opinion about my cooking."

Michelle took a bite of chicken. "It's delicious, marvelous."

"It's my recipe. I mixed the spices that go into the breadcrumbs myself, and the cream sauce is my unique creation."

"I'd say you're a talented chef. Is the swiss cheese imported? It tastes expensive."

"Yes, it's French. I like it, too."

They ate with occasional glances and warm smiles toward each other. Michelle had somehow restrained her right eyebrow from popping up. Having her eyebrows even made her appear soft and approachable. Maybe she had been doing facial exercises.

They cleared the table together and washed the dishes. Jeff spooned out bowls of cinnamon ice cream, and they went out on the balcony to sit and watch the coming of darkness.

"Do you want to talk about the fourth of July?" Michelle asked.

"There's nothing to talk about."

"I came by the office the other day to talk, but you were busy with Sister Mary Catherine and those little boys. I felt proud of you, Jeff."

Jeff took a breath and sat up straight. "It's no big deal. They needed dental work. I'm a dentist."

"Yes, but you were giving of yourself and your talents. Your compassion was showing."

"Sister Mary praises me. She says I'm a saint. It's good for my image."

"Whatever, I'm still proud of you."

"Are you ready for me?"

Michelle laughed. "Abrupt, to the point. Yes, I am."

They stood up, embraced, and walked hand in hand into the bedroom. Jeff lit a half dozen candles and arranged them around the room, so there was flickering, soft light everywhere. He turned and began undressing Michelle, her blouse first.

"I have a surprise for you," Michelle said. She slipped out of her slacks and twirled around in the candle light.

"Wow, your purple thong. It looks great."

"There's more." She stepped out of the thong, put her hands on her hips, and turned to face him. "I got a Brazilian bikini wax. They call this a landing strip."

Jeff grinned, undressing. "I can see why. It looks like a good place to land."

Later, after an hour or so, Jeff was resting on his elbow next to Michelle, her head and shoulder propped up on a pillow. His chest and stomach rested lightly on her, and he had nuzzled his face into the nape of her neck. It was subtle. Jeff moved his right pectoral muscle upward, pushing Michelle's left breast up as he whispered about the moonlight on her skin. It took several minutes and slow, incremental movements, but her breasts moved into general alignment. Michelle sighed and let him have his way, but his action broke her mood for the night.

"Let's get in the Jacuzzi," Michelle said.

Jeff got up, stretched, and padded into the bathroom. He leaned over the Jacuzzi, turned on the water, and adjusted the temperature. Michelle came up behind him, reached down, cupped his right testicle in her hand and pushed up.

Jeff straightened up. "Hey, what are you doing?"

Michelle giggled. "Making you even. The right one is too low."

"You need to let go."

"Okay, Jeff, I just wanted you to know how it feels to get rearranged. Weird, don't you think?"

Jeff grabbed a bottle of lotion and threw it against the wall. He turned and shouted. "That's standard for men's balls. It's not normal for tits and eyebrows. You're deformed, I'm not." His face got red, and he jabbed his finger at her. "Don't you get it?"

He stormed out of the bathroom, threw on some clothes, and headed to the door. As he marched out the door, and just before he slammed it, he turned and shouted, "This is not going to work out. Let yourself out when you're ready. I've done all I can."

Jeff drove to the Sandia Casino. He won fifty-five hundred dollars, drank too much, and vomited a couple of times in the bathroom. It took all of his will power to stuff the money in his pocket, leave the casino, and drive home. The ice cream bowls and spoons were washed and put away. There was a note on the table. "You're right—not going to work. It's hard to love a selfish bastard."

Jeff wadded up the note, threw it in the trash, and put his newfound cash in the freezer. For the next two weeks, Jeff worked hard and took Ambien so he could sleep. Rachel stood by while he self-medicated with Nitronox every other night. He called Ben and arranged a time to go by and see him on the next Saturday. Late on Monday afternoon, a new woman, Veronica, arrived at his apartment.

10

$\mathcal{V}$eronica happily complied with all of Jeff's desires. She was suited for him because her only task was to please him, because their relationship was secret, because she presented an exquisite anatomy, and because she was a custom-made, life-size doll.

Jeff grinned at Ben halfway through their session. "My Veronica is beautiful."

Though perhaps unusual, Ben had agreed to help Jeff with his recent dreams and insomnia and anxiety, and remain his friend. Jeff would never see any other psychologist, and Ben believed he could help him. Being with Jeff this way was better than no help at all.

"Veronica listens to my every word, and she never judges anything I say or do." He put his hands behind his head and leaned back. "She says I'm handsome and a great lover."

Ben leaned forward in his chair, frowning. "This is a weird development, Jeff. When did you get her?"

"She arrived last week. I ordered her a month ago. Michelle didn't seem to be enough, and one night I got on this website and the next thing I knew I had ordered Veronica.

"How much did you spend?"

"She was seven-thousand dollars. I had to put four-thousand on a credit card, but she's worth it. I hit a good blackjack hand and paid the other three thousand."

"Do people know? Was she delivered to your office?"

"No, she came to the house late in the day. The UPS driver said the box weighed eighty pounds and wondered what it was." Jeff shifted in his chair. "I told him I won a doll—a beautiful doll, a reward from the universe for my many talents. I don't think he believed me, so I told him it was an exercise machine."

"This is not progress, Jeff. You're four-thousand dollars more in debt, you're gambling, and you're isolating again. Remember? You were going to get the credit cards paid and get out and meet people—other professionals, conferences, continuing education. What's going on with you?"

Jeff rubbed his hands together and then squeezed them between his knees. "I'm bored, nervous. I need something to do with myself. Sometimes I'm not sure who I am. Work is not enough, Ben."

"So now you're obsessing with Veronica?"

"I wouldn't say obsessing, but we have been spending a lot of time together."

"Okay, tell me about her. Let's see where you're going with this."

"Well, I chose all her features, so she's perfect—what I want."

"I'm listening."

"I was assigned to an expert doll counselor. He helped me design her. Veronica has red hair, white-pinkish skin, number three nipples, grapefruit size breasts, a flat stomach with a slight pooch, and red pubic hair. It's astounding, Ben. Each single hair was implanted and then curled. Her thighs, knees, calves, ankles, and feet come from an athletic design, as though she's a regular cyclist. She's perfect in every way."

"So, the factory has artists?"

"Yes, good ones. Veronica has a rounded face, soft cheeks, thick stretchy lips with a slight smile, a Romanesque nose, and a smooth forehead beneath fluffy red bangs. Her green eyes sparkle—large size number one—and light green eyeshadow covers her eyelids. Her anatomy is correct beyond my wildest imagination."

"You mean her private parts?"

"They designed a removable orifice system—can be taken out and washed."

"Realistic?"

"I don't know how they did it, but it is a stretchy silicon foam and conforms no matter what position she's in."

"I gather you've tried her out?"

"Veronica and I have made love three times since she arrived, once with her sitting on top, once from behind, and once with her legs pushed up and knees on her shoulders. Tight and springy in all positions. There's even a hand-held air pump, and you can tighten her up if you want to. An engineering marvel, that's for sure."

"Jeff, this is bizarre—seems to be about you and full control, right?"

"Could be, but I haven't had an urge to go casino, and the salesman said I deserved to have someone like her. He said it's a special man who does well with dolls. I'm unusual, Ben, don't you see? She tunes up my vitality."

"We're about out of time. I suggest you keep a detailed journal about you and Veronica. We can go over it at our next session. I want to have our sessions be formal, and we can be friends outside the office."

Jeff stood up. "Thanks, Ben. It seems like you care."

"You're right. I'll see you in two weeks, Saturday afternoon at four."

Jeff hurried home to get another UPS package. He had bought an array of extra clothes and perfumes for Veronica. He dressed her and posed her differently each day so he could fulfill his preference when he saw her—on Monday and Tuesday he placed her near the counter in the kitchen, perfumed with Victoria's Secret Rapture, a warm Bulgarian rose, amber, and musk scent—naked except for a little apron. On Wednesday and Thursday, he posed her on the love seat in the living room with a short skirt and sheer nylon blouse, her breasts smelling of Bath by Bobbi Brown, a fresh out of the shower scent. Then for the weekend, he kept her posed on the bed in sheer lingerie with her legs open—her thighs and tummy smelling of Carnal Flower by Frederic Matte, a sweet, musty, and alluring scent that came alive when he closed his eyes. Why play blackjack at the casino when you have Veronica? He could come home anytime in any condition in any mood and Veronica was there, waiting, without judgment and ready to listen to his every word without interruption, poised to bring him all the pleasure he could muster.

Sometimes he propped her up and stood naked beside her in front of a full-length mirror. "Hey, look here Veronica. This should make you smile." He loved watching her admire his rippled muscles, his hint of tight abs, and his strong shoulders. Also, he liked to watch TV with Veronica sitting beside him, his hand resting between her thighs, under the electric blanket. He was sometimes annoyed that it took a couple of hours for her to warm up to body temperature, and she didn't hold her heat well. He loved stroking her smooth skin with his face resting in the nape of her neck. "This is a perfect friendship, Veronica. You're my kind of woman. No demands—always there for what I need." He mused about a new innovative design that generated internal heat, but that doll was two-thousand dollars more and had to stay plugged in—kind of unnatural. For now, an electric blanket had to do.

Just after four on Saturday, Jeff appeared for his therapy and sat down in the quiet of Ben's office. "I have a confession to make."

Ben opened his notebook. "Okay, let's have it."

"I went back to the casino. Lost about thirty-seven-hundred dollars and then I left. I haven't been back."

"I thought your friend Veronica was keeping your home fires burning?"

"Well, she was, but her skin is just too clammy and cold."

"You said she's perfect, a woman who admires you and listens to your every word. What happened?"

"Sometimes she can be annoying."

"You said she thinks you're a great lover. How could she possibly be annoying?"

"Well, there's not much variety. And my desire wanes against cold thighs."

"Cold thighs?"

"Yes, you have to take the time to warm her up with the electric blanket. Hard to be spontaneous."

"But she meets your every need, right?"

"Not so much anymore. Her nipples are chewy and taste like plastic."

"How did you feel when you decided to go play blackjack?"

"Excited, eager."

"Because you might win?"

"Yes, or maybe because I might lose—playing—that's the point. I like to stay right on the edge of what's going to happen."

"Does it always feel like an adrenaline rush?"

"Always—I love it."

"What made you stop?"

"I ran out of money. My credit cards are maxed out."

"Seems like a bad strategy—running out of money. We need to talk about impulse control and your obsession with self-satisfaction. Where do you think that comes from?"

"Well, I didn't get enough of what I need as a child, and I haven't gotten enough in any of my relationships. It is not an obsession. I deserve it. I'm unique, Ben. I need more than other people, and women don't understand."

"You're unique, all right. Some force drives you, Jeff. You're not in charge of your impulses, judgments, or your emotions. I've said this before, but let me repeat it. You don't know who you are or what motivates your life. We've got to work on how you see yourself. I know there's a compassionate, good-hearted man in there somewhere behind your shadow. Self-centeredness does not serve you well, Jeff. You are a man among people, not an island. Pardon the analogy, but bees exist for the good of the hive. You live in a community, Jeff. Self-satisfaction only goes so far."

"I do pretty well. I don't think I need to change that much."

"Pretty well? You're broke, you work long days to make your office function, you've maxed out your credit cards, and you can't sustain a relationship with a woman—even a doll. You call that doing well? If I were a worker bee, I'd toss you out the door. You have no purpose."

Jeff stood up and looked at Ben. "Men like us need things. You know that Ben."

"You may be right about that. Can I ask you a question?"

"Sure."

"Do you ever have childhood memories?"

"I didn't have much of a childhood."

"How's that?"

"I think I was born grown up."

Ben smiled, putting his hand to his chin. "When did you start to mature, age thirteen?"

"I've been mature for as long as I can remember."

"Sometimes men get stuck along the way, around age fourteen or fifteen."

"Have you met men like that?"

Ben put his hands on his head, fingers interlaced. "Almost everyone, except you, of course."

"I just keep moving forward. I can't afford to get stuck."

"Remember how drones get stuck? Their sex organ is barbed. What if you are stuck in that age thirteen world?"

"Not likely. Please stop talking about bees? I hate them. They're the reason I'm in this situation."

"Bees caused your life to fall apart?"

"They ruin everything, or the women do."

"You think that?"

"The bees are out there. They fly out ahead of me and screw up my life."

"Or the women do?"

"I'm looking for perfection, Ben. Women pretend they're perfect, lure me into a relationship, and then I find out they don't measure up. They are the ones to blame, not me. Of course, I could have better judgment, but I get lonely."

Ben shrugged and looked at the clock. "Guess we're out of time."

"Okay, I've got to get going anyway."

Ben put his hand on Jeff's shoulder. "Are you all right? I hammered on you."

"I'm okay." Jeff grinned. "Most of what you say is bull shit anyway. "

"Are you going to the Casino?"

"Yes."

See you again in two weeks?"

"Okay, Saturday at four."

Ben made some notes, thumbed through a couple of books, straightened up his desk, and went to IHOP for an omelet and pancakes. It was dark when he pulled into his driveway in Algodones and saw a large box on his front porch, balanced under the porch light on a furniture dolly. He wheeled it inside, closed the door, and opened the front of the box. Veronica was dressed in sheer pink lingerie and was holding a note in her hand. "Hello, Ben. I've had a bath." Ben took Veronica's hand, wheeled her into the house, and turned off the light.

11

*D*ebbie Gonzales was conceived in Destin, Florida on a white, sandy beach on a pile of tan beach towels on Sunday, July 15, 1979, under a half-moon and a hundred yards from a blue, slack tide. *Bad Girls* by Donna Summer was playing on a small portable radio. Her mother, Florence, neither a bad girl nor a sad girl, and her father, Carlos, were naked, swim suits bunched up nearby. Florence noticed some people walking by in the distance, and they watched for a moment, but she didn't tell Carlos and kept her legs hooked around him so he wouldn't notice. She took an extra quick breath and felt a little shiver. Being exposed, but not seen, excited Florence, and she didn't know any of these people so what the hell. They were far enough away that they couldn't see anything specific, just two bodies getting it on. She suppressed a giggle thinking of Carlos's tight little butt shining and bumping up and down in the moonlight. She wanted to get pregnant, so this was their fifth time this week.

Florence was a determined and controlling woman, traits she shared with her mother, Bernice, who in turn had inherited them from Florence's grandmother, Bertha. Bernice's teen years were awkward because Bertha hovered over her and kept her clothed with long dresses, leggings, high collars, long sleeves, and clunky shoes, a source of embarrassment in the face of her friends. Florence vowed that if she ever had a daughter, she would allow her to embrace her femininity without fear.

Carlos's father, Francisco Gonzales, had recovered from alcoholism in his early years, settled down, and found Carlos's mother, Maria, while playing guitar in a band in Miami. Maria auditioned as a singer, and her voice was so smooth and mellow that she started work that night. Whenever she sang, Carlos found himself daydreaming about her beauty and had to take a deep breath so that he could focus. Carlos's grandfather, Alejandro, was also a daydreamer. He found work as a commercial fisherman, and few people knew that when he watched the seas, he was not keeping a sharp lookout. Rather, he was daydreaming about his wife Luna's smile, her soft, warm body in the early morning, her enchiladas and refried beans that she fed to the family, and her bright blue eyes. In his drinking years, Alejandro had daydreamed about other women and his exploits, but Luna's loving presence kept all of that in the past. Debbie's lineage featured strong women and daydreaming men—all of whom were kind and helped people whenever they could.

Rachel had missed a few of her Narcotics Anonymous meetings, and she was feeling squirrely after helping Jeff with his repeated Nitronox evenings. She decided to go to a Saturday night women's' meeting at the rehab center on Jefferson. Rachel recognized a few people from her other meetings, but there was one she couldn't place. After the meeting, she approached a tall lively woman with a bright smile and bouncy breasts.

"Hi, I'm Rachel, Rachel Curry. Don't I know you from somewhere?"

"Yes, I'm Debbie Gonzales. We worked together at Presbyterian for about a month. I seem to remember that you left."

"Yes, and with no choice—a diversion program, my second time. I've been clean for two years now."

"Two years for me also. I got my MBA from the University of Phoenix in a cocaine fog. It was fun, and I finished, but I probably fried my brain. Big C is not my friend."

"Are you still at Presbyterian?"

"No, I went to work at the Heart Hospital about a year after you left. I'm doing well. I got moved into Administration, so I've been working extra."

"Do you like it?"

"I didn't realize how different Administration is from just being an RN. Now I'm in charge of all the nurses, and their payroll and benefits, and their continuing education, and their work schedules. I hire and fire as well. New relationships, new rules, new boundaries, new accountability—I've been feeling swamped every day like I need a little bump, so I've been going to more meetings."

Debbie was tall, about five feet eight inches, and on the edge of a plus-size. Her bright blue eyes sparkled from her small oval face. She had high cheekbones, and her full, defined lips gave the impression she had a permanent flirtatious smile. Her black hair was cut short, even with her chin, and framed her face. She wore jeans and a blue jersey tee shirt, and her cleavage was quite apparent, though not inappropriate. Her skin on her face, upper chest, neck, shoulders, and arms was the color of mocha honey, skin so smooth and soft that she might as well have been wearing a sign that said, "caress me." Rachel took a step toward her and asked in a quiet voice, "I don't mean to be forward, but are you seeing anyone?"

Debbie tipped her head, smiling. "Occasionally dating around. No one steady. Why do you ask?"

"Well, I work for a dentist, Jeff Corley. He's single, just came out of a relationship, and I know he would like to meet you. He's handsome and lonely."

"What does he like to do for fun?"

"He's focused on himself and his stuff—you know, his car and his apartment, but I know he likes to gamble. He goes to the Casino often, but he says it's because they have a good buffet and it's hard to cook for one."

"I like to gamble, too, and I've limited myself to twenty-five dollars whenever I go. About the same expense as going to a movie."

"So there's a start."

"I need to have my teeth cleaned. Maybe you could work me in for an appointment?"

"Sure. I'll give you a call. Is an early morning time best?"

"Yes, I need to be downtown before nine."

Debbie came on the following Thursday. Rachel was finished cleaning Debbie's teeth by eight-thirty.

"Dr. Corley, could you come in please?"

He extended his hand. "Hello, I'm Jeff Corley, and you must be Debbie Gonzales?"

"Yes, it's nice to meet you."

"I'd like to check you over." He used a small mirror and looked at every tooth, both sides. Debbie's bright blue eyes followed his eyes as he worked, trying to avert his eyes from her white scoop neck blouse and visible mounds pushed up by her white lace bra.

"Rachel did a great job cleaning, and your teeth are in great shape. There's one tiny cavity we could fill, but let's wait and keep an eye on it."

Debbie got up out of the chair, pulling down her short skirt. Jeff, and for that matter, anyone, would notice that her womanliness was evident for anyone who wanted to see, and her countenance made her seem appropriate, right on the edge of proper.

"Thank you, Dr. Corley. I'll look forward to seeing you again. I'll leave my business card with Rachel at the front desk."

Jeff smiled his broad, white smile. "Good to meet you."

Debbie smiled over her shoulder as she left. She uses her features, which has given her an advantage in her new job. It had been six weeks, and already she's discovered that the women who don't judge her and admire her taste in clothing, become part of the team. Women who find her too sexy, too exposed, and judge her to be on the make, tend to self-select out of their jobs and look for ways to move on. Men who admire her body and also respect her abilities, gather around and help her to get ahead and succeed. Men who admire her beauty and try to move in on her, get nowhere. They find themselves rejected and soon on the outside of her sphere of trust.

Her greatest supporter at the hospital is an older heart surgeon who told a colleague, "Debbie Gonzales is remarkable—RN and an MBA. She's smart, filled with compassion, has good judgment, and, let's face it, easy on the eyes. People admire her femininity, but her body soon takes a back seat to her intellect. She's a leader. We're glad she's here."

When Debbie got to her office, she called the florist and had a little bouquet sent to Rachel with a note, "Thanks for the excellent cleaning." Her mother had told her, whatever else you do in life, make sure you are always kind and that you always help people—help people and find ways to appreciate them and give them hope. That's what life is all about. Kindness and hope.

The next week Jeff called Debbie and asked her out on Saturday evening.

"Hello, Jeff. I'm backed up with work until evening. Could we meet about six? I've been sitting all day. Let's do something active and then eat somewhere."

"You mean like a hike in the mountains?"

"No, that's too active."

Jeff thought for a moment. "How about Cliff's Amusement Park? We could grab a bite at Pelicans and then go on a few rides at Cliff's. Pelicans' baked salmon is tasty."

"Okay, I'll meet you at Pelicans and leave my car there. We can take your's to Cliff's."

"Okay, then, I'll look for you at about six."

They split a light dinner of baked salmon and chips and talked about work. Jeff wore a new light blue polo shirt, chinos, and polished loafers without socks. Debbie had on a white scoop neck jersey top, ironed blue jeans, and blue and white tennis shoes. They took Jeff's BMW to the amusement park. Jeff bought two Saturday night family passes, and they started off with a ride on the Cliff Hanger. Debbie got off first after the ride.

"I'm sure glad we had a light dinner. Any more and I'd of lost it all."

Jeff laughed. "You've got that right. We should walk around a little while."

They went on the Side Winder, got wet on Rocky Mountain Rapids, and sat by the New Mexico Rattler for a while drying off. Part of Debbie's wet shirt had stuck to her front, and Jeff seemed delighted with what he saw. Debbie didn't seem to care what showed.

"Are you ready for the Rattler?" Jeff asked. "It scares everyone."

"Sure. Let's do it."

Breathless, hair flying out from her face, Debbie grabbed on to Jeff's arm and pulled him close. He pushed himself to her even tighter and smelled her vanilla shampoo and body wash. Her muscles were firm, and she was stronger than she looked, like a tennis player with a surprisingly fast serve. There was a sturdy ripeness about her. Debbie turned and looked at him, her green eyes flashing.

"Hold me, Jeff, hold me."

He moved even closer. "I've got you," he shouted as they rounded a quick turn. And the end of the ride, they got off a little shaky. Jeff guided her to a concession stand. "Want a Coke?"

"A small one."

They strolled around the park, sipped their cokes, and sat on a park bench.

Debbie held Jeff's hand. "Having fun?"

"This is great, Debbie. We've got time, let's hop on the Demolition Disco."

"The bumper cars?"

"Yeah, we can see who's the best driver."

They made a couple of rounds bumping into strangers, and then Debbie caught Jeff with a smack on the side that spun him around. He followed her and pushed her into the rail, turned her around, and with a big grin hit her car head-on with a bump that shook their teeth and snapped Debbie's head forward. She gritted her teeth and came after him, pushing him into two other cars that were side by side, and he spun around between them. The ride stopped, and they walked to the side.

"Want to go again?" Jeff asked.

"No, that's enough. Let's sit down."

Jeff put his arm around Debbie. "This is turning out well—who would've thought an amusement park would be a good first date? Glad I thought of it."

"You seem competitive, Jeff. You shook my teeth loose."

"Well, fortunately, you have a good dentist."

"No, I mean you are quite competitive."

"I like to win."

"Even at bumper cars? I'm just a little ole' woman driver. Why would you compete with me?"

Jeff took her hand as they walked. "You're attractive, Debbie. I guess I want to show you I'm worthy."

"Worthy of what?"

"Your attention, your admiration."

"You have my attention, but my admiration requires a lot more than bumper cars."

"Would you like to come to my apartment? There's a full moon tonight over the Sandias—we can watch it from my balcony."

"Do you have coffee?"

"Four or five kinds. You can choose."

"Okay, let's go get my car, and I'll follow you."

Jeff ushered her in, turned on the lights, and introduced her to Budgey. Debbie walked straight to the kitchen and opened the top of the coffee maker. "What kind of beans are already in here?"

"Major Dickinson Columbian."

"Oh, that'll be okay. Is this where you add the water?"

"Yes. Use that little pitcher and the small faucet—that's the filtered water."

Debbie leaned over to fill the pitcher and her scoop neck opened wide. Jeff looked down her shirt, and then as she adjusted her top, his warm eyes met hers for a moment. Debbie turned away, poured the water, and started the coffee. The grinder whined, and coffee aroma filled the kitchen.

Debbie walked from the kitchen. "Okay if I look around?"

"Sure, I'll turn on some more lights."

He stepped ahead of her and turned on the lamps in all three bedrooms and the vanity lights in both bathrooms.

"Wow, three bedrooms. Do you have a roommate?"

"No, I like lots of room and the best view. I might have guests stay over. You never know."

She wandered around. "I like your Wilson Hurley landscape—breathtaking. Excellent taste, but all your other paintings are nudes."

"I like Steve Hanks."

"So do I, but he's done water colors of children, mothers, and daughters, families by the sea. Why only nudes? I mean if you were still fourteen or fifteen, but you're all grown up, aren't you?" Debbie smiled at him.

"Let's just say I'm fascinated by the female form. They are all signed, limited editions."

"Pardon me for saying so, but your taste seems one dimensional. Where's the balcony?"

"Over here, behind these curtains."

Jeff pulled the drapes and slid open the glass door. The moon was just rising over the north side of the mountains. Debbie came out and took his hand. "Takes my breath away. The moon seems alive, don't you think?"

Jeff turned and leaned in to kiss her. She turned her face as he kissed her cheek.

"Coffee's ready. Should I bring you a cup?" she asked.

"No, I'll get it. Cream and sugar?"

"Please."

He returned with coffee cups on a small tray with cream and sugar in crystal bowls.

They sat down, sipped coffee, and watched the moon.

"I'm a little worried," Debbie said.

"About what?"

"I have this new job, you know, and I'm expected to understand how to manage people. I have the credentials, but no experience. I'm not very confident."

"Anything I can do? I'm sure you'll catch on. How hard can it be to manage a few people?"

"There are about thirty nurses and assistants, a couple of I.T. people, medical equipment vendors. They all have schedules, days off, requested vacations, continuing education requirements, OSHA and safety regulations, Human Resource employment guidelines, and protocols, and that's just the beginning. Lots of moving parts and some people resent that I'm a woman manager."

Jeff squeezed her hand. "Don't worry about me. The last thing I dislike is you being a woman."

"Oh, I know, but I was wondering if you know anyone, you know, from a dental or medical practice who I could talk to, perhaps even a mentor."

"Not right off hand, but you can talk with me. How hard can it be? Get me a few books on medical management, and you can track along with me. I'm smart, Debbie, and I'm quick to learn. At least you could bounce your ideas off of me."

Debbie got up and took the coffee service to the kitchen. Jeff followed.

"We've only just met, Jeff. I don't want to impose on you, so don't buy any books or anything. I'll call you next week, and maybe we can have lunch. I'll feel more confident next week after a few more days on the job."

"Sounds great. I'd love to see you again."

Debbie walked to the door, turned and shook Jeff's hand.

"Okay, it's time to go. Thanks for dinner and amusement park. Thanks for the coffee and the moon."

In the morning, Jeff heard a loud knock on the door. He ignored it, waited until he started coffee, and then opened the door and peeked out. He looked around and retrieved an envelope stuck to the door. It was a three-day notice, three days to get caught up with rent plus the late fees or move out. Those bastards. In a couple of years, he'd be successful enough to buy the whole fucking building. He poured coffee and sat in the kitchen with a legal pad and a pencil. Rachel said she'd wait to cash her paycheck from Friday. The water company wanted payment for two months by Wednesday. His dental supplier said he could continue purchasing, but it would have to be COD until he caught up, and his payroll tax deposits were a week overdue. He had three-hundred dollars in the freezer. He got dressed and decided on Buffalo Thunder Casino. He hadn't been there for a while, and none of the dealers would remember him. He paused for a moment, thought about his plan, and then called Ben.

"Are you busy today? I'm in a jam and need to talk with you."

"Can you come by over the noon hour? I'll be in my office."

Jeff paced around his apartment, and then went to the gym and ran on the treadmill for a while until he was out of breath and covered with sweat. His smell disturbed him—acrid, lemony, like the smell of fear. He showered, dressed, and splashed on his Escape Cologne. Then he stopped at Starbucks on his way to Ben's office.

"Hi Ben, here's a half-café soy latte and a bagel." Jeff took a quick sip of his red eye."

"Sit down, Jeff. What's going on with you?"

"I met a girl. Her name is Debbie, and she's breathtaking. We went to Cliff's Amusement Park last night and out to dinner. She's a nurse with an MBA and works at the Heart Hospital. She could be the one, Ben. I'm fascinated."

"That's great, but what's that look on your face? You're covered up with anxiety, right?"

"I'm dead broke, I've maxed my credit cards, and I got a three-day notice for my rent. I've got to have three-thousand dollars by Tuesday afternoon, or they're going to throw me out."

"Let's think about that. How bad would that be? You're in a luxury apartment you don't need. Maybe you should downscale."

"If I don't pay, I won't be able to rent anywhere else. Landlords always need references."

"Could you find a roommate, move in with someone else who has an apartment? Save some money for a while?"

"You know I can't do that. Hey, I was on my way to the Casino, but I promised to call you before I went again, remember?"

"I'm glad you did. At least you can think about some options."

"Ben, I was wondering. What happened to Veronica? Do you still have her?"

Ben grinned. "I was wondering when you would ask. Believe it or not, she's in her shipping box in my storage unit down on Central."

"Did you have a chance to get to know her?"

Ben laughed out loud. "I thought about it, but I was worried about who she had been with before. You never know. This culture reeks with STDs."

"Maybe I could sell her. I've got eighty-five hundred in her. What do you think she would bring?"

"Gosh, I don't know. Maybe you should put an ad on Craigslist and see if you get any calls."

"Sure, let's give it a try. Can we use your computer? We could do it right now."

Ben went to the Craigslist site. "What do you want to say?"

"Try this: *Gorgeous, female, one-owner, adult doll. Redhead. Anatomically perfect. Available now. Albuquerque. Phone number.*"

"Sounds good, Jeff. What phone number?"

Jeff walked to the door. "I'll be right back." He went to his car and got a small box out of his trunk and returned. "I've got this burn phone—you know, for emergencies. Let's use this."

"You had a burn phone in your car?"

"I keep a couple of them. You never know when you might need one."

"We need an email address."

"Okay. Here's one we can use to verify."

Within twenty minutes the ad was posted. As of one, Jeff had received six calls and had arranged to meet buyers at Ben's storage unit.

"I'll be free after four. We can meet people at five. Maybe you'll sell Veronica before they day is over. Good thinking Jeff. Avoid the Casino, and get rid of an asset you don't need."

Just after five, a white Cadillac drove up the aisle to Unit #117, Ben's storage unit. A middle-aged man stepped out of the car. He wore cowboy boots, creased Levi's, a light-blue western shirt with pearl buttons, and a light gray cowboy hat. He sauntered over to Jeff, Ben, and the open door. Veronica was standing in her shipping box dressed in a sheer, pink, nighty.

"Is this the little lady?" he asked.

"I named her Veronica," Jeff said, "but she won't mind if you change her name. She's one-owner. I had her at home for only a couple of weeks."

"What happened, did she get mad and you had to put her out of the house?"

"No, I met another woman, the real kind."

He touched Veronica all over, and then leaned down and lifted her nighty.

"She seems well-designed. Is she as realistic as she looks?"

"Perfect. I designed her. Those private parts can be removed and washed. Silicon. Springy in all positions." Jeff opened a suitcase. "She has a wardrobe. About five-hundred dollars worth, and I'll throw in all her clothes. I've got eighty-five hundred in her, but I'll take six-thousand."

"That's pricey. She's a cut above anything I've seen before, but that's out of my range. I have two other dolls, and I just want to add to my collection. Think I'll keep looking around."

"What would you offer?"

He reached into his back pocket and took out a fold of hundred-dollar bills.

"I've got thirty-eight hundred here. You can have it all."

"Can you add a thousand? Make it forty-eight hundred?"

"Sorry, son, thirty-eight hundred is the offer."

He put the money back in his pocket, turned, and walked toward his Cadillac.

Jeff looked at Ben. Ben nodded.

"Wait," Jeff said. "I'll take it."

They loaded Veronica into the trunk of the Cadillac and counted out the money.

"It's all here. You got a good deal," Jeff said.

The man drove away. Ben closed the storage unit door, and they drove back to Ben's office.

Ben got out of the car. "Way to go, Jeff. Now, take that money to your landlord and pay the rent. Give the rest to Rachel on Monday so she can pay some bills. I know you have other stuff that is pressing."

"Thanks, Ben. You know what? I don't even miss her."

"Good progress. You made some headway today."

"I guess so. I'm going to call Debbie."

"Be careful. It sounds like Debbie may be fanning."

"Fanning? Is that a bee thing again?"

Ben laughed. "Worker bees produce a pheromone and send it out to bees away from the colony. It is like a homing beacon. Calling her might be like calling home. Once you get the pheromone in your nose, you are on your way."

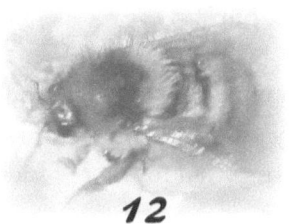

12

$\mathcal{R}$achel followed Debbie out of the NA meeting, and they paused in the parking lot.

"Gosh, this is the second time I've seen you this week, Debbie. Are you doing okay?"

"I have to pick up on my meetings. Lots of pressure at work and stuff I don't know how to handle."

"It sure is great to see you. How are things going with Jeff?"

"Has he said anything about me?"

"He tells me you're voluptuous and smart. I think he likes you."

"He's attractive, but there's something about him that bothers me."

"What's that?"

"I know he's a friend of yours, but addicts must be honest, so please don't take offense. He's self-centered, arrogant to a fault, but he hides it well. He has good manners."

"Yes, he can be a gentleman, but you're right, and he gets what he wants."

"How do you get along with him at the office?"

"Our friendship is complicated. For some reason, he rescued me. I was on leave from my hospital job on a monitored diversion program. Had to drop urine three times a week. I told him the truth in an interview for a job, and he hired me."

"Did he want something?"

"I figured he did. We had one intimate encounter, but it didn't work out because I prefer women, but what the hell, I thought I'd give it a try."

"You prefer women? That must have bruised his ego."

"I think so, but I told him it wasn't him, and, of course, he had already come to that conclusion."

"Well, it's clear he didn't fire you."

"Nope. I've been with him two years now. He trusts me to manage his work life. He's kind of like a brother."

"What's your greatest challenge?"

"Handling the money. It's like a roller coaster ride, you know, up, down, sometimes out of breath. I've gotten to where I hide money from Jeff for emergencies, like my payroll taxes."

"From what I see, he lives way beyond his means."

Rachel laughed into her hand. "You've got that right, but he always pulls a rabbit out the hat. The rabbit lives at the casino. I would think that your budgeting skills would be good for him."

"You mean if he'd listen to me."

"Well, yes, there's that."

"Do you have time for coffee? There's something at work I want to ask you about."

"Sure, I'll meet you at Starbucks—that one on Eubank and Candelaria."

They both bought Frappichinos and sat in the overstuffed chairs in the corner by the windows.

"Debbie, I know I can trust our anonymity, right?"

"No worries, what's going on."

"I think I have a drug problem with my staff. There are two nurses on the night shift that use all their sick time, show up late, and are often forgetful with their charting."

"Warning signs, for sure."

"Yes, but how do I catch them without upsetting the whole staff? You know the ropes. I'm new, and most of the nurses and assistants have been there for three or four years."

Rachel frowned. "My boss made a terrible mistake. He didn't tell anyone. He was sneaky, manipulative. I think you should tell everyone that you won't fire them for drug use and that you provide a diversion program to help people with problems. Then start random drug tests for all the staff."

"Won't that put people off?"

"Sure, but the clean nurses won't mind, and the dirty ones will watch their step. Good nurses don't like to work with addicts. It's too risky for patients."

"What else?"

"It's a headache for a while, but you should show up now and then at shift change and supervise the drug inventory count. Bore down on it.

Check signatures. Let everyone know how important it is for you."

"I could do that. I get to work early anyway. If I get the inventory under control, what's the sneakiest way nurses get narcotics?"

"I'm ashamed of this, but they get it from patients, IV drips and injections. Simple. You put saline in the syringe, chart that you administered, say, morphine, and then take the morphine home in another syringe."

"How do I catch that?"

"Now, that's a real project. You have to monitor the patients' pain level, say at eight in the morning and check the chart. Look at the history. If the pain level is high, you've got a suspect."

"I probably need a trusted ally. I can't do that all by myself."

"That works. Your RN ally can be the one who watches. Best if she's a charge nurse."

"I have someone in mind."

"You won't be able to catch everyone, but the word will spread that you watch things. You'll flush out someone who needs help, and the others will see that you live by your promise to help. Just give them one chance, though."

Debbie nodded, and then made some notes on a notepad she took from her purse.

"I feel like a hypocrite. I'm an addict trying to catch addicts. I used blow to get where I am."

Rachel reached over the table and took Debbie's hand.

"I know, but that was then, and this is now. Besides, it's your job, and you're beginning with compassion—you want to help your staff."

"Thanks, you've been a great help."

As they walked to the parking lot, Rachel paused.

"Do you mind if I ask you a personal question?"

"No, go ahead."

"Have you slept with Jeff yet?"

"No, I'm not sure what to do about that. He's a gentleman, but pushy."

"Well, according to him, you'll be in for a real treat when it happens."

"A treat."

"He fancies himself a lover in the first degree, a ten."

"I don't do well in a new relationship. I'm awkward when it comes to sex."

"Well, just get the first time over with, and you'll know what to do from there."

Debbie grinned. "Gosh, Rachel, you do look out for him."

Rachel hugged Debbie's waist. "It's a little selfish. Jeff is easier to manage at work when his sex life is satisfied."

"No one told me that in management classes."

"Yup, the first principle of management. People are easier to manage when they have healthy sex lives. It just can't be in the workplace."

Debbie got in her car and lowered the window.

"Thanks for your advice. I'll see you Sunday night at the meeting."

Rachel watched Debbie drive away, and a hint of desire welled up. She was sorry that Debbie was straight.

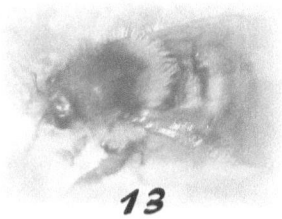

13

*J*eff picked me up at my place, and we went to the Santa Ana Casino in Bernalillo for their buffet, our first real date. I felt stunning in light blue spaghetti strap jersey top and black slacks and matching black pumps. I had just gotten my hair done, and it framed my face the way I like it. Jeff wore a green polo shirt, creased blue jeans fresh from the cleaners, a light tan jacket, and his penny loafers without socks. As we walked into the casino and Jeff bought buffet tickets, I think we appeared to be an item, a vibrant couple ready for a delightful evening. I liked the feeling. I hadn't been on an official date with a handsome man in a long time. And, he smelled good, mysterious.

There were dozens of choices, but we both chose salmon, snow peas, squash, and fresh spinach salad.

"We have similar tastes. I like that," Jeff said.

I smiled and thought about his Steve Hanks nudes.

"Maybe so. Wilson Hurley and salmon and a roller coaster so far. Stay tuned for more."

We ate our salads, and then Jeff asked me about work.

"I've had a good week. I put some protocols in place and initiated a new employee drug program."

"Did you know what to do? I wish you had brought me those textbooks."

"I thought things through myself, talked with a few people and got advice from an experienced person who knows about drug programs."

"A management expert?"

"Let's just say an experienced management consultant."

"You should bring me some books. It won't take me long, and I can help you."

After key lime pie, we circulated among the blackjack tables. Jeff watched the tables, found one he liked, and we sat down together. I bought my self-imposed limit of twenty-five dollars in chips, and Jeff started with one hundred dollars. With Jeff's coaching, I soon had two hundred and was grinning from ear to ear. Jeff was down to fifty dollars."

"Wow, this is fun, Jeff."

Jeff bought a couple of gin and tonics.

"Can I just sit here and not play for a minute?" I asked.

"Sure. Enjoy your drink."

Two Aces landed in front of Jeff.

"It's double-down time. I need to borrow fifty dollars. You'll get it right back."

Jeff hit two blackjacks and scooped up his two-hundred in winnings. He stood up, gave me my fifty back, and picked up his drink.

"Come on, let's change tables."

Within an hour, my stack had grown to two hundred fifty, and Jeff had two thousand. I put my hand on his.

"We're way ahead, Jeff. We should stop now."

"Hey, I'm just getting started."

"Not me. I can use this two hundred fifty for my utility bills. I'm going to wander around. I'll find you later."

Jeff found Debbie in the lobby.

"Can you spot me one hundred dollars? I've had a run of bad luck."

"You lost your two thousand?"

"Yes, but I'll win it back."

I gave him a hundred. "Can I have the car keys, please? I'm going to sit in the car and listen to the radio for a while. It's so noisy in here that I have a headache."

I had just gotten settled when I saw Jeff approaching the car. He got in the driver's seat and slammed his palm against the steering wheel.

"Shit. Not my night."

"Did you lose the hundred?"

"I was ahead a thousand. Pisses me off."

"I can see that. I've still got one hundred and fifty dollars. That's what we started with, and we had a nice dinner. No reason to get angry."

Jeff took a deep breath. He turned to me and grinned with his teeth gritted. His face turned red.

"You're right. Let's go to my place for a glass of wine. I picked up a couple of bottles of Burgundy."

I remembered what Rachel had said. Just get the first time over with. Then you'll know what to do. I guess tonight might be the night. Why the hell not?

We drank the full bottle of wine. He put Smoky Robinson on the stereo and started to open another bottle.

"I've had plenty, Jeff. No more for me." I looked him and smiled.

"This might be a little forward of me, but would you like to take a shower? There's a new fluffy, terry cloth robe hanging in the bathroom. '

"That's not a little forward, Jeff. That's *screaming* forward."

"Well, maybe so, but might help you relax."

"I am relaxed."

Usually, at this point, I would have laughed, stood up, put my hand on his chest, pushed him away a few steps, and then left the premises. I don't like pressure, but here we go.

"You know what? I am a little chilly, and the hot water will feel good." I stood up, pecked him on the cheek, and went in the bathroom.

"Save some hot water for me."

I showered, slipped on the robe, folded my clothes and left them on top of the dressing chair.

"Come on in here and rest easy for a minute," Jeff said. "I'm next."

Jeff was not at all modest undressing and walking to the shower. His lean muscles rippled as he walked, and although he didn't have a six-pack, his waist and hips were slender and tight. He looked like a Greek statue. Maybe Rachel was right. Maybe this would be a treat. I turned off the lights and stretched out under the down comforter. Jeff laid down beside me, warm and spooning, his hand caressing my breast.

"What happened to the lights? I've been waiting for weeks to see you. You are beautiful."

"That's not going to happen, Jeff. We don't know each other that well. Wow, what's that cologne?"

"My Noir Extreme, for special occasions, like now. Exotic?"

"Exotic, that's the right word."

I was surprised and delighted. Jeff's perception of himself as lover sure matched the reality of the next half-hour. He was slow, gentle, thoughtful, and practiced in women's anatomy. This should have been a treat, but for some reason, I still don't understand, it wasn't. I pulled away.

"What's the matter?" he whispered. "Are you okay?"

"I have to be honest, Jeff. I'm not feeling much of anything down there, or anywhere for that matter. Is that too honest?"

"Not feeling anything?"

"No, there's just nothing happening. Why don't you go ahead with what you need, and then we can cuddle for a while."

I accommodated Jeff, and then he sat on the edge of the bed.

"Do you have any idea what's wrong?" he asked.

"There's nothing wrong," I said. "I'm just not feeling any passion. It's not you."

"Yes, I know it's not me."

"It's lovely to be close to you, Jeff. We can try another time."

Weird. I just want to get this first time over with, and I can't even get started. I got up, dressed in the dark in the bathroom, and walked into the kitchen. I've probably ruined this friendship. Maybe I did too many lines of Mr. C. Maybe I've burned out some brain cells. I wanted to slap myself.

"Let's have some coffee and then you can take me home."

14

*J*eff and Debbie spent every weekend together in August. On the last Sunday of August, Debbie took Jeff to the Quiet Life Assisted Living center to meet her mother, Florence. They had lunch in the dining room and then drove up to Sandia Peak for an outing. Jeff was a gentleman, but agitated. He was discontent. They had made love a half-dozen more times, but each time he was accommodated instead of pulled into the throes of passion. At Debbie's request, Jeff went on a picnic with them on Labor Day and then worked on repairing a crown for Florence on Wednesday. They tried again on Friday night, and then again on Saturday evening.

Muted light from the parking light showed little beads of sweat on Debbie's upper lip. Jeff rolled over on his back, and Debbie put her hand on his chest. "Would you like it better if I just pretend?"

"No, that wouldn't be better. Besides, I can tell if you fake it."

"Just be patient with me, Jeff. Aren't you happy with how I treat you?"

"Well, as far as that goes, you are everything a man could ask for, but sometimes, like tonight, it feels a little mechanical. Maybe if you looked in my eyes, or something. But, hey, who's complaining?"

"It's getting better. I know it is. We light a candle now, and I'm comfortable with you seeing me sometimes."

"I know, and I can't get the sight of you out of my head. I'm distracted all day long. I can smell you on my chest and arms for hours, like cinnamon and vanilla."

"It's just body lotion. Please, Jeff, have a little hope. Maybe it won't be long, and the volcano will erupt."

On the following Tuesday morning, Jeff got a call from Debbie at the office.

"Hold on a minute," Rachel said. "I'll get him on the line."

"I need to see you after work."

"You sound like you've been crying. What's going on?"

"Can we go somewhere? I'm scared."

She came to the office, and Jeff drove them up to the base parking lot of the La Luz Trail.

"Okay, now what is it?"

Debbie cried. "Florence is dying."

"What?"

"She had horrible pain, they took her to the ER, they did a scan, found stuff on her pancreas, did a biopsy...she's in the last stages of pancreatic cancer. The doctor said he couldn't understand why Mother hadn't complained about pain sooner. She said it wasn't that bad. She thought it was arthritis in her back."

"Prognosis?"

"Bad. She might have eight weeks. They put her in the nursing unit at Quiet Life. I'm afraid to go see her by myself—I don't want to fall apart—will you go with me?"

"When?"

"This evening."

"Okay, let's a bite to eat at Flying Star, and then I'll drive you down there."

It was just after mealtime at Quiet Life. They walked by the dining area, down the hall into the nursing unit, knocked on 224. The name tag said, "Florence Sanchez. Please knock."

Florence was lying on her back, eyes closed, breathing with some difficulty, and moaning. Debbie held her hand, and Florence opened her eyes.

"Oh, Mother. I'm so sorry."

Florence squeezed her hand. Jeff sat in a chair by the bed. They sat quietly for a while, although Jeff was squirming. A nurse came in.

"You must be Debbie Sanchez, Florence's daughter, right?"

"Yes. I'm her daughter."

"Her admission file says that you are her medical power of attorney. Is that still the case?"

"Yes, I don't think she changed anything."

"You will need to meet with our placement office. It's down the hall, across from the dining area."

"You mean now? It's after hours. Is someone there?"

"Yes, every evening until eight. It is about seven fifteen now."

"We'll come in a few minutes."

Florence would not let go of Debbie's hand.

"This is bad," she whispered. "The pain..."

Debbie let go of her hand. She took the chart at the end of the bed and began reviewing it. The pain had come on fast as if a tumor had burst. Florence was admitted to the nursing unit yesterday, and already she was receiving ten mg of morphine every four hours. Her pain still broke through. Any more morphine and she could stop breathing. The notes said "terminal pancreatic cancer—prognosis six to eight weeks." Debbie knew that the only thing they could do now was to keep her as comfortable as they could until she died.

The nurse returned, and Debbie watched as the nurse injected Florence's morphine dose into the IV tube. Florence took a couple of labored breaths and closed her eyes. Jeff walked with Debbie to the placement office.

"I'm sorry," the placement manager said. "As you can see, she needs to be moved to a hospice facility. We can't handle her here."

Debbie cried. Jeff handed her a tissue from the desk.

Debbie nodded. "Yes, I understand. I'll look into it and be back tomorrow."

They drove to Jeff's apartment and sat on the couch.

I didn't know what to say. I had a few quick memories of my mother in a hospice bed as Debbie grabbed my arm and snuggled close. I felt lost. I had absolutely no idea of what to do with a sad woman. I felt a slight urge to help. I was uncomfortable, irritable. Should I hold her? What should I say? I just met Florence. Hey, sad she has cancer, but what does that have to do with me? I eased myself up, went into the bedroom, and called Rachel.

"Can you meet me at the office?"

"Now?"

"Yes, I need your help. I feel nauseous, dizzy."

"Okay, I'll be there in thirty minutes."

Jeff covered Debbie with a quilt and drove to the office. When Rachel arrived, Jeff was already in the dental chair with his mask on and Nitronox running through the hose.

"Are you in a bad way?" Rachel asked.

"I'm a mess. Debbie's mother is dying. Just found out. What am I supposed to do?" He tipped the chair back and inhaled a few times.

"It sounds like to care about her."

"I sound that way? I'm not sure what that is."

"Yes, you sound that way. Just lie back and breathe."

Jeff stayed in the chair for more than an hour. His pulse and blood pressure returned to normal.

"That's enough Jeff. We don't need you disappearing into Netherland."

She took off his mask, and he opened his eyes. She helped him stand up and move into the waiting room and sit back down.

"Don't do anything, Jeff. Just be with her. Don't tell her anything. Don't try to control anything, okay? Think of it this way. Whenever you have the choice, do *not* be yourself."

Jeff chuckled. His eyes, mouth, and cheeks appeared so relaxed that he could have been a child.

"Don't be me. That's funny. I think I can do that. Not well, but a little."

I drove back to his apartment. Debbie was asleep in bed, still in her bra and panties. My God, she was beautiful. I stood and stared. She was self-conscious of her near plus size, her small side rolls, and her jiggly tummy, but all I could see was an abundance of a soft woman who felt like heaven when I was next to her. I stripped naked, unhooked her bra and slipped it off, spooned in behind her, and buried my face in the hollow of her round neck. I inhaled her skin smell, cinnamon, and honey.

He woke up at six and heard the coffee pot finish its cycle. Debbie was in the kitchen in her bathrobe.

"Good morning, Jeff. I called the office. I'm taking the day off. Can I talk with you?"

Jeff sat down in the kitchen in his undershorts as Debbie poured him coffee.

"Not quite awake. Give me a minute, here."

He rubbed his eyes and drank half of his coffee.

"I have something to ask you, Jeff. I'll understand if you say no. I'm almost afraid to ask."

"It's okay. Ask."

"Your view of the mountains is outstanding. You have a lot of room. My apartment is dark and dreary. Can Florence come here until she dies? She would be attended by hospice nurses twice a day. You wouldn't have to do anything."

A lump formed in my throat. I felt faint. I covered my mouth with my hand.

"You think that would be a good idea?"

"I'll come over before you come home, straighten up, and get dinner ready."

"Will you go home at night?"

"No, silly, I'll sleep here with you, in your bed."

"When do the nurses come?"

"In the morning after you leave, and in the afternoon before you get home. They change her, feed her, give her meds, and check her vitals."

Don't be yourself. Don't be yourself. Rachel, I'm doing the best I can.

He reached out and touched Debbie's hand.

"Gosh, what can I say?"

"Mother has some money, so I would expect to pay the rent and utilities."

"Of course, Debbie. Of course. Move her in."

Debbie went to Jeff, held his hands, stood him up, opened her robe, put his arms around her back, and hugged him, rocking side to side, pushing her ample bare breasts against his bare chest.

I've not felt this warm in a long time...all the way into my heart. Weird.

"Thank you, Jeff. You're an angel."

An angel? Okay, Rachel, I did it. I did not be myself.

15

*J*eff walked into Ben's office, coffee and pastry in hand.

"Good morning, Jeff. Thanks for the coffee. What's being going on with you?

Jeff sat down. "I met someone."

"Why am I not surprised?"

"Debbie Gonzales. She's a knockout. Rachel thinks I care for her. She's warm and soft and sweet, and she'll do anything I want. The only problem is that she doesn't feel much."

"How's that?"

"She has a passion problem, you know, down there."

"She doesn't like sex?"

"She seems to like sex okay, and she likes to be close, but she says she doesn't feel much."

"Do you mean non-orgasmic?"

"I guess so. Debbie asked me if I would feel better if she pretends. I told her, no, I could tell. I want her passion to be responsive. I want to be the source of her pleasure."

"A month ago you would have told me you didn't care, as long as you were getting your needs met. You didn't seem to care with Michelle, and of course, and not with your doll, Veronica."

"I don't know. I just want to turn her on."

"Okay, but turning her on might take some time. Don't obsess. Maybe she has to get to know you better. Just relax about it. What else is going on?"

"Her mother is dying in a hospice bed in my living room. Debbie is a Medical Administrator at the Heart Hospital and makes good money. She's so soft and beautiful I can't stand it. I've been using Nitronox a lot. She's paying the rent until her mother dies. We went to the casino. I lost two-thousand. She doesn't like my Steve Hanks nudes."

"Whoa, slow down. I can't follow you. I've not seen you agitated like this for a long time. Take a breath, one thing at a time."

"Okay, Debbie Gonzales. She's gorgeous. When she hugs me, I feel different, like someone cares about me. She's smart. RN and MBA. Her mother, Florence, was diagnosed with end stage pancreatic cancer and has maybe six weeks to live."

"So Florence is at your apartment? You wouldn't ever let something like that happen—huge intrusion into your space, like having a bumble bee in a honey bee hive."

"I know. I don't understand it myself. Debbie makes dinner and sleeps with me. The hospice nurses take care of Florence, or Debbie does."

"Are you comfortable with that?'

"More or less. It's just strange. Feels like I have a rope around my neck and someone is pulling, but I don't know where."

"It doesn't seem at all selfish. Maybe something is pulling on your self-centeredness."

"Maybe."

"But then again, she's paying the rent and sleeping with you—making dinner, too. But how do you feel when you see Florence in bed?"

"A little sad, like when Mom died."

"This is a real stretch for you, Jeff." Ben smiled. "Maybe there's hope for you yet."

"Yeah, thanks."

"What about the Nitronox? Why are you using more?"

"Like you said. I'm agitated, restless. It helps."

"Does Rachel still watch out for you?"

Jeff grinned. "Yes, indeed. She's the attending nurse."

"Good. I don't want you hurting yourself. Do you ever feel stuck in your altered state, in your dissociation?"

"I don't feel stuck. I come right back when we turn off the gas. It's like I'm hovering above myself, watching myself calm down, and then I slip back down into myself."

"Watch out for rabbit holes. You might end up in wonderland."

"I could use a little wonderland. Reality is too intense right now."

"Okay Jeff, so let's see if I get it. You care for a beautiful woman. You've displayed what appears to be compassion. Your substance abuse has increased.

You're restless and discontent. You have a home cooked dinner every night, and you sleep next to a gorgeous woman."

"I guess that's about it."

"Sounds like you've elevated Debbie's status. You care for her. She reminds me of a queen bee in one of my hives. She's the reason the hive exists—royalty. You know that, right?"

"A queen bee?"

"Sure. You go to work and come home caring for her. You want to serve the queen. You want to turn her on. You want to treat her like royalty."

"Not the bees again, Ben. Please."

"I'm just an ordinary psychologist, Jeff, but I'd say you've entered a time of change. It will be hard to go back."

"What should I do?"

"You don't know? You always know what's right and what to do."

"Well, I don't know about this."

"If you're asking me, I'd say relax, enjoy the ride, stay open to whatever's next, and may the force be with you."

"Well thank you Obi-Wan Kenobi—the Jedi master."

"You're welcome, Luke. Keep your light saber handy."

16

*T*wo weeks transpired with predictable days, hospice nurses, spectacular sunrises, quiet afternoons, delicious dinners, and quiet, alone time for Debbie and Jeff. As the days passed, Florence's pain increased. She was receiving her limit of narcotics and risking respiratory failure. She had a Fentanyl patch and twenty mg liquid morphine every four hours, yet her pain still broke through. The frequency of her moaning increased each day and night until it was keeping Debbie and Jeff awake at night. For Debbie, Florence's moaning was torment.

"What else can we do about her pain?" Debbie asked often.

The answer was always the same.

"We're doing all we can without risking her death," the nurses said. "Her respiration is way below normal. We shouldn't let it go any lower."

"But she's in agony."

"Yes, but all we can do is keep her as comfortable as possible."

"Are you positive? There must be something else."

"I'm sorry. We can only administer palliative care. More morphine would border on euthanasia.

"But she's out of her mind with pain. It's torture."

"This is out of the ordinary," one nurse said, "but I do know someone who just might be able to help. She's outside the medical community. Some say she's a medicine woman. Others call her an alternative healer."

"Who is she? Can we call her?"

"Her name is Elissa Fortuna. We are out of options. I'll call her."

17

*I*t happens in unusual ways. Sometimes it happens during passionate, mind numbing sex, but other times it happens with gentle touching, massage, quiet listening, or even honey bee stings. It all depends upon the intensity of the pain in the man or on the severity of cuts on the arms of women.

Elissa Fortuna doesn't know why, but she has the gift, or perhaps a curse, of taking on the chronic soul pain of suffering men and women. She absorbs their pain, drinks the pain, indeed becomes the people, suffers their pain as they become one reality, and then sends the pain away and shines light into the black hole of their darkness. The soul pain does not come back, and both Elissa and the man or woman experience a poignant lightness of their very being. At thirty-six, an attractive single woman and a joyful bee keeper in Albuquerque, she has lived inside the transformation of at least three dozen men, not counting the nine high school boys whose broken home lives moved them to despair. She lifted over a dozen teenage girls into a peaceful place, and they stopped cutting themselves. Her light had transformed their despair into hope.

Oh, how she wished her mother had lived to see her gift at work and to help her understand. She would have told her that for both her and the men and women, the scary pain process is sensual, ineffable, mysterious, and sometimes a strange mixture of dull throbbing pain and exquisite pleasure. We cannot know it in the usual sense. We can only grok it. She would have told her about the profound memory that was formed in a high school English class when she read Robert Heinlein's *Stranger in a Strange Land*. That day she wrote a quote on her notebook. "All that Groks is God." It became her oath. Soon after, she realized that she was brought into this confusing, brilliant, mysterious life, with all its forces and facets, to capture pain from the hearts of troubled people, young and old, soaking pain up and rinsing it out into a netherworld that she couldn't see, even in her mind's eye. She regretted that her mother could not be with her to behold the new paths she had forged for her friends, and the success of her purpose, her destiny. Why did she have this gift? Is this why had her mother said her life would be magical?

Elissa was conceived on a musty old couch in the back office of an exotic dance club just off the Interstate in Albuquerque where her mother Louise Fortuna worked as a bartender. A small, slender man with a bright smile, sparkling blue-green eyes, light brown skin, and black hair with a single braid down to his shoulders, came into the club one Saturday night, sat at the bar, ignoring the exotic dancers in favor of a delightful conversation with Louise. He introduced himself as Jitin, a traveler from Nepal who said he was here on an education visa, a journey for his mind and heart. He came to the bar at the same time each Saturday night for several months, and for Louise, became the most sympathetic listener she had ever met. She thought he might be a holy man. His eyes opened wide with interest as she talked about when she and her mother ran away from her father. He was not shocked when she talked about her mother's jobs here and there when they lived in an old car. Through moistened eyes, she told about her mother's addiction to heroin, her turning tricks for drugs and her mother selling Louise's virginity. She shared her deep, painful secrets about failed relationships with mean men and her never-ending heart breaks. She emptied her heart to him. She was accustomed to listening to customers, but Jitin listened to her and became her spirit companion as she poured out her life to his warm and willing soul.

"None of my boyfriends have ever stayed around for more than six months. They love me and leave me. I make bad choices. I don't choose good men. Can't figure it out."

Jitin leaned over the bar, touched her hand and spoke. "It is not about choosing the right man. First, you must know what you want to do with your life. Then you can find a companion who loves to do that with you."

She smelled spicy sweetness on his breath and leaned toward him. "That's a huge question for me. What do I want to do with my life? What can I do? God only knows."

"Do you want to be rich?"

"Money is important to me, but I only need enough to live on—I would like to live well without financial worry—I guess like most people."

Wrinkles formed up beside his flashing eyes as he smiled. "Well, you are already beautiful. Do you want to be more beautiful?"

She adjusted her bra. "Thanks, but I'm fine the way I am."

"What excites you? What makes your soul arise? What makes you come alive?"

She looked up, touching her chin. Who is this man? Her chest warmed. Was she reddening? Could he see her blushing? "Why do you want to know? Where is this going?"

He held both her hands. "I've come a long way to meet you. I must be with you. You are on the path of my destiny."

She felt a shiver in her lower back and squeezed her cheeks. "Well, that's a new one. Never heard that line before. After all our time together, are you going to hit on me now?"

"I must sound foolish. It is not a line. I am your friend." He reached into his pocket and pulled out a small photograph. "See, here's a picture of you from three years ago, taken at the Albuquerque airport. My teacher said I should come here and search the nightclubs until I found you."

She squinted in the soft light. "That's me, all right. I went to San Francisco to meet a boyfriend, an ex-boyfriend. He liked to handcuff me—a real prick. Why would someone take my picture?"

"My teacher saw you in his meditation dreams and said that you would be at the airport on that Monday morning. He asked the student to take your picture. You see, my teacher prays without ceasing and looks for people who can create goodness and light beyond themselves. I know that sounds odd, but he is a carrier of goodness, and he has taught me how to be a carrier as well. He has a gift of discernment, and he finds people who will move humanity forward with the power of the spirit within them. He told me that your purpose is to bear a child whose destiny is to help others escape from their pain. You have the spirit and power of creation within you. God has filled you with his spirit, and your strength can bring goodness into the world. You have no evil in you, but you need to manifest your creative energy so that your goodness can spread out upon others. You must bear a child."

Louise gazed above his shoulder. "Excuse me. I'll be back in a few." She came out from behind the bar and made her rounds of all the tables, taking orders. The one waitress was caught up in conversation with a table of four men—working on a large tip no doubt. Louise returned, scurried back and forth, made a tray of drinks, and delivered them with a smile and a spring in her step. She could feel Jitin following her with his eyes. She had light brown hair that bounced when she walked. She wore tight orange shorts, high ankle boots with knee-high orange socks, and a light beige spaghetti strap jersey top. Her pink bra straps were alongside her spaghetti straps, and her shorts were low-cut, showing a slim midriff and lower abdomen beneath a narrow, silver belt. She had a piercing in her navel, and a tiny silver angel dangled from the ring. Her eyes were light brown, and her lips were thin and pleasant and turned up at the corners. Her high cheek bones, rounded chin, and subtle smile gave the impression of innocence. She wore ear rings that were silver angels, matching the one dangling from her navel. Men often asked her if she was one of the dancers, begging her please to hop up on the stage, grab a pole, and show her stuff. "No, I'm a bartender and a damn good one. I don't take off my clothes except when I go home."

She returned and leaned on her elbows again, face to face with Jitin. "This is so weird. What do you mean by creative energy? You come here every Saturday night and listen to me talk about my scattered rotten life, and tonight I'm filled with power, the power of creation itself? Are you crazy?"

"My teacher says there are only a few people who have no evil in them, and the power of creation that is in them need only be released. He has sent me to show you how you can produce a healer, a carrier of light that changes the next generation and produces offspring whose light will draw suffering people to the healing presence of God. Your destiny is to bear a child who can lift the pain of the world, one person at a time. You are a woman with more power than you can imagine."

She tipped her head and grinned at him. "Jitin, this is freaky. You think I'm one of those people?"

"My teacher does, and I believe him, so I am dedicated to this mission. You are part of my destiny, like others I have met. The seeds of goodness fill the trail behind me, and the path ahead carries light to the next generation. The healing light comes through you and others like you." He smiled, eyes flashing. His face seemed to glow. "You hold the power of creation. You only lack a tiny seed, a seed I've brought you as a gift."

She felt warm again in her lower back, and her midriff turned pink. "So, how does this happen?"

"We find a way to merge the power of the second chakra, to harness our energy. Could we find some time alone tonight after work?"

She grinned again, stood up tall, put her hands on her hips, and shook her hair. "The second chakra? Now you're messing with me."

"Yes, the second chakra, the sacral chakra. Chakras are whirling energy centers. The sacral chakra contains the energy of creativity, our sense of well-being, our pleasure—and yes, our sexuality." He pointed. "It is there, about two inches behind that little angel and a little farther down."

Louise laughed. She leaned close to his face—he was frowning and had an intense look about him. She almost touched his little nose with hers. "You're serious, right?"

"This is the most important event in your lifetime. Empty vessels like you are rare. We must make our energy swirl, our chakras entwine. You will receive a gift that will change your next generation, and your life will become peaceful. You will find joy. Your descendants will be free of evil within them, spread goodness, carry light every day, and relieve the pain of the world."

"So, Jitin, what do I have to do, fuck you?"

"Please don't be crude. When our energies merge, a newness will appear in your life. The energies are rooted in our sacral chakras, so we will have to mix in that way, yes, but it is not selfish or greedy. It serves a higher purpose. It is a sacred gift to you and your offspring."

After the bar had closed at two, Louise took Jitin's hand and led him into the back room, the office with the old musty couch. She spread a sheet out on the sofa, kicked off her boots, slipped off her shorts and panties, and flopped down on the couch with a smile on her face and her arms outstretched, hands beckoning. "Okay chakra man, get your stuff over here and let's see what happens. Can I enjoy this or do we have to be serious?" She giggled, then became wide-eyed as he undressed. His thin body was lustrous and seemed to glow with a white aura and flashes of light in the semi-darkness.

"We will feel the warmth and intense pleasure—that's natural. But we must remember the purpose and the gravity of the merging of chakra energy. You will conceive a child, but the world will surround you with care, and you will be all right."

He was slow, strong, deliberate, and tireless. He whispered strange, gentle words into her ear, and the energy of his loins drew her up to him with a steady drumbeat, over and over and over. After a while, her body tingled from head to toe, and her hips felt warm, flush and yielding. She cried out with little murmurs as a crescendo of whirling heat energy pulsed and quickened in her and between them. She wrapped her long legs around his waist, hooked her heels together, and squeezed him even closer. "It's now, Jitin, it's now." He slowed but did not stop until she sensed the surging flow of his energy filling her. She nuzzled into his neck. She could hear the siren of a lone fire truck and cars out on the Interstate nearby. His still-glowing skin gave off an intense fragrance of fresh cinnamon and frankincense. He kissed her lips, her cheeks, and her ear. "You are with child now."

She murmured. "No, I don't think so. My time of the month comes in a couple of days. I'm not ovulating."

He moved side to side. "Yes, I can feel it, grok it."

"No, it can't happen now." Louise slipped her hand between them and below her navel, and, in between her breaths, she felt a quivering warmth and goose bumps on her stomach. "I feel the heat. It is almost like a sunburn inside me."

"The sacral chakra, the beginning seeds of goodness. They are taking root."

"Jitin, I'm afraid. What if I am pregnant? I'm just a bartender. I don't want to be a single mom like my mother. I can't let that happen again."

"The world will surround you, comfort you, and take care of you. I will send you money for your baby. You must stay calm and open to the flow of energy. Your goodness will attract all of your needs."

"Now what, are you going away?"

"Yes, I will continue on my path."

"Will I ever see you again?"

"No, but I will be with you, and I will guide your child in the spirit."

"Jesus, I can't believe we did this—and I let you—like a fool. See what I mean? I always make stupid choices."

"No, my darling. You have chosen well. Be patient, and you will see."

Jitin dressed and touched her cheek. "I must go now. May your life shower God's grace upon others and bring them joy and peace." He closed the door.

Louise sat up, crossed her arms, and watched the shadows out the window from the lights as cars raced by. A high-speed motorcycle whined, and she could still smell his frankincense. She shook her head and bit her lip. There goes another one. He was so kind, but now he's gone. They love me. They leave me. Soon she fell asleep on the couch. When Louise awoke, she felt drawn to a new spiritual place. A compulsion to attend her well being seized her and drove her into action. Over the next few days, she quit her job at the bar, scrubbed her apartment until it shined, and went to work in a cafeteria where she wore a maroon uniform with a white apron. She gathered her hair under a hairnet, and she smiled as she pointed out healthy choices for patrons. One benefit of the job was that she received two meals a day. She made healthy food choices, did not drink any alcohol, slept well, and sought prenatal care often. She felt shrouded in mystery, but her compulsion for self-care continued. If nothing else, she would have a healthy baby.

To her surprise, the week her baby was born, a girl, she received a fifty-thousand-dollar wire transfer to her savings account from a bank in Nepal. She named her little girl Elissa, after the Hebrew name Elisheba, God is my oath. Louise never spoke of Jitin but told Elissa that her father was a holy man who had died just after Elissa was born. "Your life will be magical," she said, "and your father told me that your destiny is to relieve pain and bring joy and light into the world, one person at a time."

"But why? Why me?"

"I wish I could tell you. There are some things we can never know—not until we do them. Just know that I believe you are divine, and I will love you forever."

20

*D*ebbie met Elissa at the door. "Hello, I'm Debbie, Florence's daughter. Thank you for coming."

They walked to Florence's bed. Florence lay on her back with a clean white sheet covering her up to her waist. She wore a light pink hospital gown, and her gray hair was loose beside her face on the pillow. Her eyes were closed and squinted with pain. Her breathing was slow and labored. Her right hand was on top of the sheet, and her fingers moved, scratching the sheet. At the end of every third breath, she moaned and twisted her torso. Though heavily sedated, the pain broke through all the combinations of medication that the hospice nurses had tried. She was up to 40 mg of liquid morphine every four hours. More morphine or another Fentanyl patch could be euthanasia.

Elissa sat down beside the bed and took Florence's hand. Elissa put her other hand on Florence's stomach on a place above her pancreas. She sat for a moment, and then tears came to her eyes.

"This pain is exquisite, worse physical pain that I've seen for a long time. I'll come back this afternoon and do what I can."

"Thank you," Debbie said. "Anything will help. I'll be glad to pay your fee."

"Oh, I don't do this for money," Elissa said. "This is my calling. Relieving pain is why I exist."

After lunch, Elissa returned with a small canvas bag. She took out an array of marking pens and laid them on the bed—the colors of the rainbow in order, red, orange, yellow, green, blue, indigo, and violet. She folded the sheet down a little and took Florence's hand.

"Florence, I'm Elissa. Debbie has asked me to come and see you. I am going to try some things to ease your pain. Will that be all right with you?"

Florence squeezed her hand. Elissa opened her gown on her stomach area, making sure she covered Florence's breasts. She glanced up at Jeff. He was not looking at Florence. He was staring at Elissa. She winced and took a deep breath, looking back at Jeff.

"This might be a little chilly. I'm going to make a picture on your tummy, but don't worry. I can wash off when we're through."

Elissa took her time. She created a picture of a flower garden that completely covered Florence's stomach from one side to the other. She drew purple asters, yellow and orange marigolds, white clover, light blue cosmos, deep purple butterfly bushes, pink and white honeysuckle, giant sunflowers, and a border of flowering purple sage. Jeff, Debbie, and the hospice nurse became fascinated with Elissa's artistry. Then, with precision, Elissa drew four honey bees positioned in the garden, each above a flower, and where they formed a circle on the area corresponding anatomically with Florence's wasting pancreas. The detail on the honey bees made them look so real they could have been buzzing around the garden.

Elissa reached into her bag and took out four small jars and laid them on the bed. Each jar contained an actual honey bee. Jeff moved back and stood behind Debbie, peering over her shoulder. Elissa retook Florence's hand. "Florence, we are going to let some tiny honey bees sting you. I promise it won't hurt but for a minute, and there's a good chance it will lessen your pain. Is that all right with you?"

Florence opened her eyes and raised her eyebrows.

"Florence, would you like to see the picture I drew? It is a garden."

Florence squeezed her hand. Elissa took a large hand mirror from her bag and held it up above Florence so that she could see the picture on her stomach. There was the hint of a smile on Florence's lips.

Florence moaned, writhed, and squeezed her hand.

One at a time, Elissa placed a small, open jar over the bees that she had drawn. The live worker bee in the jar settled next to the bee drawn on Florence's skin and stung her. She flinched each time. Elissa pinched the bees after they stung to hasten their death, knowing that honey bee stings are sacrificial. Once they sting, they leave the stinger, the venom sack, and a large part of their abdomen in the person. Elissa put things away, and then placed several drops of lavender oil on the bee stings. The areas around the bites turned bright pink, then white, and then returned to the flesh tone. Elissa put both of her hands on Florence's stomach. Elissa closed her eyes and sat for several minutes. Everything was quiet except for Florence's labored breathing and moans.

Melissa shuddered. "I'm so sorry Florence. This pain is staggering, ungodly."

The room became quiet. Elissa and Debbie looked at each other as Florence moaned again, this time her cry was softer, shorter. Florence squeezed Elissa's hand, then nodded, then closed her eyes as her moans stopped and her breathing evened out.

"I don't know how long this relief will last," Elissa said. "Let's pray it continues through the night. I'll come back first thing in the morning."

Debbie stood and hugged Elissa. "Thank you, thank you."

Jeff shook Elissa's hand. "Yes, thank you." Her hand felt hot, almost too hot to touch. His hand turned white, and he felt a shudder, like an electric shock, travel through his body. He sensed a pull toward something once again, and he stepped back, a pulsing lump in his throat.

Florence's moans awakened Jeff and Debbie about five. Jeff made coffee, Debbie showered and made some toast, and they waited for the hospice nurse to arrive and give Florence her morphine. The nurse came first, followed soon after by Elissa.

Elissa hovered over Florence and repeated her ritual with the bee stings, lavender oil, and touch. Once again Florence's moaning quieted.

As she pinched the bees and gathered her things to leave, Jeff stood up.

"Let me walk you to your car," Jeff said.

He walked beside her, carrying her bag of supplies.

"Where do you live?"

Elissa paused beside her car. "I live in Placitas, Jeff. Way out near the Forest Service road."

Jeff stared into Elissa's light brown eyes. She was eight inches shorter than him. Her auburn hair shined in the sunlight as it fell on her shoulders. She wore light blue eye shadow and no other visible makeup. Her face was long, angular, and wrinkled, more so than her forty-five years would have produced, but her full cheeks and lips overshadowed any impression of aging. In fact, to Jeff, she was drop-dead beautiful, glowing, and filled with vitality. Her voice pulled at Jeff like a magnet.

"You seem to have a lot of pain," she said.

"Oh, I'm okay. I'm a little stressed. Debbie's mom dying is difficult. Haven't done this before."

Elissa put her hand on his heart.

"I feel old pain," she said. "Very old pain. It's congealed, twisted, contained. Feels like it has a life of its own. Jeff, I think I can help you."

"I'd love to get to know you, but you've got your handsful here with Florence."

"Can you get away on Sunday afternoon? Here's my card. There's a map. Say about three?"

"Well, that might be awkward."

"Tell Debbie that I see the pain in you and I think I can help. She cares for you. She'll understand. I don't want to steal you away. I want to help you."

Elissa returned each day to work with Florence. On Saturday morning, she asked Debbie to walk with her to her car.

"I gather you've noticed that Jeff is drawn to me. I've sensed horrible pain in his heart. I have invited him to my studio to see if I can help. I asked him to come at three tomorrow. I know he feels awkward, but I'm hoping you understand. I'm not after your man, just his pain."

Debbie looked into her eyes. "I can be okay with that."

"I may be touching him."

"Yes, but you're a healer. I understand."

As Elissa got in her car, Debbie noticed her slim hips and shapely legs as she stepped lightly. She was slender, and her skin was dark, the color of light mahogany. Her breasts were full and young under her loose blouse, free and easy. Elissa seemed unaware of her body as a body, and more like a carrier of some force, a container of mystery.

Later that night after dinner, Jeff told Debbie he needed to talk with her.

"Elissa Fortuna says that she sees a lot of pain behind my heart. Ben says I'm in a time of change and I ought to yield to whatever is next. Elissa invited me to her studio for a treatment of some kind. Would you be all right with that?"

"I think you should go, Jeff. It might be helpful."

"You agree with her? You think I need help?"

"There's something in there I've never understood, Jeff. Sometimes you frighten me with your intensity and your anger. You should give it a try."

Jeff drove to Placitas on Sunday, several miles past the village and on a back road into the woods. As he topped a small rise, a meadow opened up, and there was a small house at the end of a driveway. The yard was filled with flowers, and there was a fruit orchard nearby. He saw six beehives spaced throughout the small orchard. A friendly, black Labrador greeted him as he got out of the car and walked to the front door, keeping an eye on the bee hives.

"Hello, Jeff. You're right on time. Let me show you around."

They walked around the house, and she named all her flowers, shrubs, and trees with such softness in her voice that they could have been children.

"My orchard is this way," she said. "Peaches, apricots, and apples."

"Yes, I saw it," Jeff said, stopping. I don't do well with bees. They hate me."

Elissa turned her head and raised her eyebrows. "Oh, I see. Well, okay then, let's go in the house."

She invited Jeff to sit at the table and poured him a cup of tea.

"This is chamomile. It will help you relax."

There was an oversized massage table in the living room area as well as a daybed.

"Would you like to talk about anything, Jeff? I'm open to anything in your past that might help me understand. Can you remember times that hurt?"

"My father. He was tough on me, but that's about all."

"Nothing else?"

"No, except that you're so beautiful and inviting that I'm conflicted. I mean I can't believe that Debbie thinks this is a good idea." He smiled. "If I didn't know better, I'd say you are a Goddess—I'd call you the Goddess of Womanhood."

"I don't want you to get the wrong idea, Jeff. Your flirting will be to no avail. My calling is to remove pain, not to become a partner or a lover or a one-night stand. I realize you're conflicted. Most men are when a woman offers to relieve their pain. I understand how your brain is wired."

Jeff kept smiling and put his hand on hers. "Okay, for now, we'll just leave it at that. What's next?"

"Please take off your shirt and get up on the massage table on your back. Please don't talk. Just try to feel what happens."

Jeff removed his shirt, flexed just a little, and then climbed on the table. Elissa stood beside the table with warm oil in a dish on a small side table. It smelled of eucalyptus and rosemary and lavender. She dipped her hands into the oil and dripped a copious amount on Jeff's pectoral and heart area. Then with both hands, she began massaging his heart. Gentle at first, then up and down pushing motions with vigor and strength. Jeff became short of breath from the pressure. He closed his eyes. They were wet with tears. He began to stretch and moan. She increased her pressure, and then stopped altogether except that her hands remained in place. Jeff felt like little Roman candles were going off in his chest from her hands to his heart, hot thrusts of energy bouncing off a wall of muscle. Then she started the pressure again. This time she climbed on the table, straddled him, and pushed with all her weight, slow, steady strokes up and down. He felt the energy increase, and the heat made his breathing shallow and fast. He became aroused from the weight of her straddle and the motion of her body. She dismounted, stood, and rested her hands on his chest.

"I've never seen anything like this, Jeff. You have that pain walled off with incredible strength. It's like there's another person in there, an obstinate man behind a wall, fighting me off with every push."

Jeff was embarrassed and put his hands on his aroused condition.

"Oh, don't worry about that, Jeff. Most men have their hormones out in front of their pain. Your sexual pursuits have become your best defense against feeling your pain. You're like my drones out there in the hives. You would value your breeding more than your life. You should put on your shirt and have some more tea. That's all we can do today, but you should come back next Sunday."

Jeff sat, drank some more tea, and then scurried by the orchard to his car. He waves at Elissa as he drove away. Jeff pumped his fist. *Yes! I've found the perfect woman.*

Elissa repeated her treatments the following two Sundays. During the week, she reduced Florence's pain to a tolerable level even as Florence lingered and got closer to the end. Debbie kept up the routine knowing that the end would come soon, herself becoming sad, despondent, and even more unresponsive. "Jeff, this is not the time. Just hold me. I need your support."

At work, Jeff often fantasized about Elissa. He knew she was the one, but he was miles from getting there. She was professional, Florence was dying, Debbie was sad and tired, and Rachel had become impatient with his increased need for Nitronox.

"It's almost every night, Jeff. I have a life. I need time at home to myself. If you want, we can cancel afternoon appointments, and I can watch you then. Of course, if you do that, you won't have enough money to run the place."

"Okay, how about this. Schedule more of your cleanings in the afternoon, and I'll go in the other room by myself. You can keep an eye out, and we can still bill for the cleanings."

"Whatever," she said. "At least I can get home at a decent hour."

On Sunday, Jeff awoke from a luxurious dream about Elissa, went in the bathroom, and looked at himself in the mirror. He was smitten. No doubt about it. She was the one. How could he make this happen, for her to succumb to the obvious? He loved her, cherished her, and would do almost anything to be with her all the time. He knew she cared for him. She'd been laughing at his jokes, lingering with her touch, and becoming more comfortable with him. His charm was working. Jeff had found his dream.

He appeared at her door at three, sat down, drank some tea, and said he needed to talk to her about something.

"We're not making much progress, are we Jeff? I'm not sure what to do. I can't seem to break through. Your destiny may be set. This life may be the only life you will ever have, and the way you are may be as good as it gets."

"No, it isn't that. I need to tell you something." He took her hand. "I love you, Elissa. You are my soul mate. I know it. What can I do to be with you—forever?"

"I was afraid this would happen."

"Afraid?"

"Jeff, you're hiding your pain. Your shadow covers it, and it feels like it's in there behind gristle and scar tissue. It fights me, it repels me at every touch, and now you're using your manhood to divert the issue to your pursuit of comfort. You see, if you become convinced that you love me, that I'm your soul mate, that you can't live without me, then I've become a force to help you deny what's real. I enable your pain instead of relieving it. We can't let that happen. Your pain is what is real, not your obsessed love for me. I want to try one more thing. Take off your clothes and get up on the table."

Oh, my God, Jeff thought as he complied.

Elissa repeated her heart and chest massage, and then straddled him and applied more weight and motion until he became aroused. She took him inside her, and began pushing, and then pulling up as she put all her weight her hands on his heart, pushing her hands up and down until his breathing became quick and short. Heavy pushing to his heart, slow pulling below. Pushing down, pulling up. Pushing, pulling. Jeff cried out and began sobbing, his chest heaving, his hips arching and legs quivering, as though fire erupted from his chest and drenched him. He pushed her away, putting his hands to his face, covering his eyes. "Get away, get away," he shouted, waving his hands around his head. "Get them away, mother. Make them stop."

After a few moments, he opened his eyes and sat up. Elissa learned forward."What did you see?"

"Bees, there were bees everywhere. They stung me."

"You shouted for your mother. Was she with you?"

"She couldn't get them out. They were in my clothes. They stung me until they couldn't sting anymore."

"We broke through a little, Jeff. The door is open."

Elissa handed Jeff a couple of tissues, and he wiped his eyes. Then he took a deep breath, stood up, and feeling like a child who wanted to hide under the covers, shook all over as he put on his clothes. He sat on the daybed with his hands on his thighs. "Unbelievable how you did that." His mouth formed a gentle smile through quivering lips. "What now?"

"Yes, I knew you would say that. Men are hopeless. Extracting pain is not sex. What now? We keep working. I think it won't be long and I can chase that tough guy out of there. I believe we can light up your shadow, shatter that wall, and you'll be set free."

Florence died the next week, on Wednesday afternoon. Debbie supervised her transport to the funeral home and signed the cremation papers. Debbie looked drawn and sad. The bounce in her step had become a shuffle. Her excitement about work had waned, and she was impatient with Jeff. Her mother was dead, the last person in the world she could depend upon, and she was worried that Jeff's preoccupation with Elissa was becoming an obsession. He didn't talk much about it, but she could almost see his fantasies as his disinterest in her seemed to increase. She spoke with Rachel after a meeting. "He's just not the same. I shouldn't have brought my mother to his apartment."

"Oh, I think he was all right with that," Rachel said, " but there's something else. His substance abuse has picked up, and he's more distracted and agitated. That usually means he's bewildered about who he is—I've seen this happen before—conflicted. I'm surprised he hasn't gone to the casino. I've been hiding money just in case."

"Does he talk about Elissa?"

"Well, I must admit, he's been talking about her more, and there's a dreamy look in his eye. She must have some power over him. I'm surprised because he never gives up his power."

"I guess so. I just don't know what's going on, but I'm going to move back to my place. Since I'm an addict and allegedly self-aware, I need to behave that way. I'm going to get a grief counselor and sort things out about my mother. I don't need a relapse. Jeff seems to add to my sadness."

"That's a good plan. A grief counselor. Get away from Jeff for a while. Go to more meetings. I'd say you're on the right track. If you get sucked into his world, you could relapse in a heartbeat."

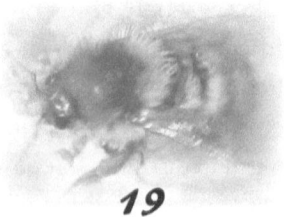

19

*J*eff went to Elissa's the next Sunday. Incense burned in a small bronze dish, smelling like smoldering pinon wood and sage. Elissa repeated the same process as before, but with one difference. This time she made him keep his eyes open and stare directly at her, not breaking eye contact. "If you don't stare into my eyes, this treatment ends," she said. "Understood?"

She used all her strength to push on his chest. She slowed her pulling motion. Drive down fast, then a slow pull. Push, pull. Push, pull with full eye contact. She watched him as he faded and then lost himself and disappeared into her eyes, totally dissociated. He sailed away and came up somewhere else, in a dark place. He smelled the musty old well house from his childhood and smelled a peanut butter and jelly sandwich he had shared with Emmy Lou. He saw the arrowhead and the gush of blood. He heard the wail of sirens; he felt the shame of his father's stare and smelled diesel fuel as Elissa stopped pushing, out of breath. Elissa's eyes came back into focus, and then a beaming smile appeared on her face, and she slumped onto his chest, breathing hard. "Jeff, I think we broke through. That little strong man in there has left."

Jeff sobbed, shivered, laughed and pounded his fists on the table on both sides of his body. He felt hot, frightened, confused. He twisted, turned, and passed out into a deep sleep. Elissa moved off of him and stood by the table with her hands on his heart. Jeff turned white, then pink, then back to his flesh tone. When he awoke, for a fleeting moment, he felt a deep sadness, as though he had missed his only chance to grasp a kind of love he could not understand. He moved off the table, his legs rubbery. He felt soggy like he just stepped out of an overheated hot tub. He could not form a coherent thought. "Can I have some tea?" Jeff asked as he dressed.

They sat quietly drinking tea and watching an orange and black finch at the bird feeder. Jeff put his hand on Elissa's. "All I know right now is that I love you. You know that don't you?"

Elissa stood up and hugged him. "There is much ahead for you Jeff. You will find love in many forms other than me. I'm a carrier, but not the answer. You're in the stream, but I'm not the rock. It's time to use your strength to gather nectar and make your honey. Remember that."

Jeff's mood lifted in her embrace, and he felt airy and lighthearted when he left. She had worked her magic, and now he could focus on them being together. Everything was jumbled up, but his path was clear. This was pure love. He slept undisturbed. In the morning, he bought some flowers and drove out to Elissa's place in the late afternoon. There was a strange car there, so he parked at the end of the driveway and walked. He looked in the window and saw a woman on Elissa's massage table. Elissa was rubbing oil on her scarred wrists, oil on her eyelids, and massaging her heart. Jeff left quietly so as not to disturb them. He left the flowers by the door.

He was elated at work and did not use his Nitronox four nights in a row. He called Sister Mary Catherine and urged her to bring more children so he could work on them. He had no urge to go to the casino. Rachel complimented him on his mood, and he brought flowers for the office. He was in love, he had found her at last, his perfect woman, and life would be good as soon as he charmed Elissa and drew her into his life forever. It wouldn't take him long—not Jeff Corley.

Late Saturday afternoon, he bought new flowers and drove to Elissa's. Again there was a strange car. He parked at the road and sauntered up the driveway, his hand and flowers swaying by his side. He looked in the window. He blinked and gasped. There was a tall, gangly, naked man on the table. Elissa was massaging his chest and heart area with both hands. Jeff shouted and pounded on the door. "Open up."

She opened it, frowning. "Jeff, what's going on? You must call before you come to see me. Can't you see I'm busy?"

"What are you doing? Who is that man?"

"This is my work, remember? You are not exclusive, Jeff. There are others in pain. I have an enduring love for you, Jeff, but right now you need to leave."

She shut the door. Jeff kicked the door frame, turned, picked up a large stone from the garden area and threw it through the window, sending glass shards everywhere. He spun around two times and ran through the orchard, waving his arms and knocking down beehives. He shouted "whore" just before he stumbled, fell, and stinging bees attacked him. Elissa heard him, saw him fall, and screamed at the swarms of bees from the house. She grabbed her bee-keeper hat and gloves, running to Jeff pulling the garden hose. Elissa sprayed him with one hand and called 911 on her cell phone with the other. She kept spraying until the ambulance arrived and transported Jeff to Presbyterian. The ER doctor estimated there were over 600 bee stings, and Jeff was critical—he may not survive. He was admitted to the Intensive Care Unit with a ventilator on a 24-hour watch, given IV fluids, antihistamines, and morphine for the pain.

I awoke swollen and bumfuzzled, bright white light and machines beep-ing everywhere. The throbbing pain had buried itself in my eyes and lips, so swollen I couldn't move them. It took all my strength to keep tiny slits in my eyes open. A face hovered over me, a face with light brown eyes. In one eye I saw reflections of my puffy face and the hose of the ventilator. I gazed into the other eye and was pulled out of myself, back in time. A rabbit hole? Rachel? I raised one hand to my face, cheeks hot and swollen. Time swirled became a torrent of wind, dust, dirt and the buzzing of thousands of bees—a roar. I put my hands over my ears, and I began sobbing. My body shivered and wouldn't stop. Enough, no more. I'm done. Darkness.

"Code in ICU" blared over the intercom. People came running.

"No heartbeat, no respiration."

The doctor rubbed the paddles together and put them on Jeff's chest. "Stand back, clear."

Jeff's body heaved. Nothing.

"Again. Clear." Nothing.

The doctor pounded on Jeff's chest.

"Is he gone?"

"Try again. Maximum voltage. Clear."

The nurse leaned down, put her lips close to Jeff's ear, and whispered.

"Again, clear." The monitor beeped.

"He's back." The doctor looked over at the nurse. "What did you say to him?"

"Just a little encouragement."

Jeff breathed shallow breaths but did not wake up.

I awoke with teeth gritted. Alive? Damn. I felt a shiver. A voice came to me, a whisper. "Jeff, we can start again." I pulled the tube in my nose. An alarm went off. A hand took mine.

"Sorry, Dr. Corley. I can't let you do that."

A sting in my shoulder. Darkness.

I woke up to a face close to mine. Had it been days? I was sweating. Again I saw into the eye. The rabbit hole? Elissa? Rachel? An eddy, time travel, sliding down a shiny uncoiled spring, round and round, dizzy. The eye sparkled. I landed in the soft dirt, laughing, crying, small. Who was I?

"Jeff, you're going to be okay. Relax."

I came back up the spring and through the eye. "What?"

"It's all right. I'm here."

"Rachel, Elissa?"

"No, Jeff. It's Emmy Lou. I'm your nurse."

Jeff smelled sweet honeysuckle and sage. "Are you an angel?"

"No, silly. I'm Emmy Lou—don't you remember me?"

"I remember... But why?"

"I think someone out there cares about us. You were dead for over a minute."

"Did God bring you?"

"I'd like to think that. I just didn't know when it would happen."

"I'm fading...."

Darkness.

A man in a white coat shook Jeff's shoulder gently.

"Wake up, Jeff. I'm your doctor."

Jeff opened his eyes. He felt his face with his hand. His swelling was down.

"You've moved past the crisis. For a while, I thought we had lost you, but you should be feeling better soon. You'll be here for a couple more days, and then I'll move you to a regular room. I've never seen a bee sting case like this. You're a lucky man."

"Hey, doc, where is that nurse that was here, Emmy Lou?"

"I don't know who you mean, but you'll probably see her at shift change."

Rachel and Debbie both stood as the doctor came into the waiting area. "Are you Dr. Corley's family?"

"Yes."

"I think Dr. Corley has moved past the crisis. The venom has worked through his system. His swelling is down, and his breathing is normal."

"Great. Thank you for the news," Rachel said.

"We'll move him out of ICU, and then he can go home in three or four days."

Debbie wiped her eyes with a tissue. "Let's get some breakfast."

They put donuts, apples, and coffee on a tray and sat at a table in the back.

Rachel sipped her coffee. "Do you think you'll try to pick up where you left off?"

"I've thought a lot about it. Two hours ago I thought he would die. He lived. Thank God. But he's got so many issues, I don't see much future."

"I know. I thought you might say that."

"I love him, and I hate him all at once. He's utterly self-centered. It's frightening."

"You know Elissa doesn't want him, right?"

"Sure, I know that, but I'm afraid if it happened once, it would happen again."

"He's highfalutin, and he's fickle—that's for sure. Not good qualities. My loyalty wears thin sometimes. I wonder if this failed suicide will change him?"

"Let's hope so, but I'm not going to hang around to find out. Mother left me a little money, and I have a good friend in Denver. She says Denver General Hospital needs nurses. They're even paying moving expenses."

"When would you go?"

"Soon. This weekend."

Rachel put her hand on Debbie's arm. "You're a lovely woman with a big heart. You know, if you ever get a yearning...."

"Don't worry. If I ever did, it would be with you. I love you, Rachel."

"And I love you. We'll always be friends. Stay in touch. Keep going to meetings."

Debbie put the corner of a napkin up to her eye. "I'll keep you in my prayers. Tell Jeff I said no hard feelings."

A nursing assistant helped Jeff sit up and eat lime green jello and beef broth, and soon after Emmy Lou came to see him. She studied him with her nurse-eye, looking for his despair, eager to assuage it. "Hi, Jeff, glad to see you are among the living."

She sat down in a chair next to the bed. Jeff propped himself up on his elbow.

Emmy Lou touched his arm. "I've wondered about you for years."

He smelled honeysuckle. "Me too."

Jeff squinted at Emmy Lou's face. She had small fat pockets under her eyes. There were gray frown lines on the sides of her mouth, and her cheeks seemed drawn and tired. Probably just age. She gave him the impression that she had endured many sad nights. Her tight lips were thin, and her smile revealed a small gap between her front incisors. She had chipped her upper right cuspid as if she'd gnawed too hard on a bone.

"Do you live here now?"

"No, I rented out the old house after mom and dad passed away and moved to Dallas."

"Why are you here?"

"For extra money. I'm working locums, part-time for an agency. Trying to save up enough to remodel the old house. I miss Albuquerque, and I think I'll move back."

Jeff nodded.

Emmy Lou moved closer. "I'm sorry things have been so hard for you, Jeff, but why would you end it all?" She smiled and raised her eyebrows. "Have you given up hope?"

He smelled sage. "I don't know anymore. I just lost it."

"Do you know why?"

Jeff put one hand on his chest. "My heart broke into pieces."

"A woman?"

"Thought she was my soulmate."

"She wasn't?"

"No, I was wrong, dead wrong."

Jeff put his forearm over his eyes."I wrote you a letter, but it came back."

"I knew you must have."

"Thirty years, Emmy Lou. Can't believe it."

"Jeff, I'm flying back to Dallas in the morning, but then I have a couple of weeks vacation. I'm coming back to meet the contractor and get the remodel started. Should I call you?"

"Call my office anytime. I'm a dentist now. I can fix that tooth."

Emmy Lou felt her chipped tooth with her tongue. "I might just take you up on that."

Jeff nodded. "The doctor says I can go back to work part-time in a week or two. I'll be there."

"You should recover quickly, now. You're strong, and your swelling is almost gone. I leave early in the morning. I won't see you again this trip." She leaned over and put her lips close to Jeff's ear. "Thirty years and I still care for you."

She stood, smoothed the back of her scrubs, and walked out the door. Jeff watched her go. It looks like her hips had settled. Might need bigger pants.

Jeff began working part time, visited with Ben three times a week, and had no urge for Nitronox or the casino. Debbie had moved to Denver to take her new job, and Elissa called a few times checking on his health. Jeff was no longer angry at her, just befuddled. One morning she invited Jeff to breakfast at Flying Star.

"Jeff, I want you to understand some things."

"Sure, I'll give it a try."

"I care for you, Jeff."

"I guess I know that, and I care deeply for you. Always will."

"Here's the truth. I am simply not able to love someone more than I love others."

"Do you just fall in love over and over?"

"Sort of. It's a gift, both a blessing and a curse. You know that I lift pain away from broken hearts and troubled souls. I feel like I'm in love when I'm doing it."

"Every time?"

"I feel love for each person."

"Men and women?"

"Yes, both. You see, wherever I go, sorrow reaches out for me. I have no choice. Remember Debbie's mom, Florence?"

"Of course."

"When I was letting the bees sting her, your fear and pain and despair filled the room and reached out to me, like two clutching hands."

"You think that's why we met?"

"I know that's why."

"But you hurt me."

"No, Jeff, I would never hurt you. I took away your old, old pain. That's what hurt, tearing it away, like dried bandages on a bloody wound."

Jeff put his hand on his forehead. "I don't know what happened. When I saw you with another man, I just snapped. I wanted to die."

"I know. I'm so sorry. I didn't see that coming. When your relief came, you were like a lost child. You didn't know what else to do."

"Maybe it's for the best, Elissa. Maybe I need to accept how things are today."

"That sounds healthy."

"Guess what? My childhood friend, Emmy Lou, is moving back to Albuquerque. We were only children, but we loved each other."

"Could you rekindle that love?"

"I don't know. She's changed."

"Time to gather nectar, Jeff. Time to make your honey."

"I'm afraid."

"Jeff, you should pursue her with all you've got. The fear will pass."

"My friend Ben says the same thing. He says don't let her abscond—that's what bees do when they leave the hive because of stress or disease."

"Yes, Jeff, I know what it means to abscond. Now it is time for dancing— that's when bees waggle around on a honeycomb to show the location of food and home sites. You need to dance. Bring her in. Show her your honey."

Emmy Lou called Jeff on Friday, and they met for lunch at Chile's.

"Jeff, I thought it might be fun to go for a walk in our old neighborhood. I need to go out to the house anyway."

"Sure, let's go. We can park up behind my old place and make our way down the arroyo."

Emmy Lou bought a couple of bottles of water, and they drove to the property and parked on the side of the dirt road. They meandered down the main arroyo and then up a branch arroyo near the old well house. The old well house was a rubble of splintered gray boards. They approached the accident location.

"Hold my hand," Emmy Lou said.

Jeff held her hand and looked into Emmy Lou's eye. It glowed with rainbow tears in the sunlight. They stood still for a while. Jeff reached into his pocket. "I still have it."

Emmy Lou looked down at the arrowhead in the palm of his hand. She took it and rubbed it between her thumb and forefinger. "You've rubbed it smooth."

"I guess so."

Emmy Lou took it from his hand and threw it as far as she could into the weeds. "You won't be needing this anymore."

"Why did you do that?"

She grinned, her eye twinkling. "Why would you need that when you have me?"

"I have you?"

"You always have."

Jeff took a breath and tipped his head. In the sunlight, Emmy Lou looked gorgeous, and that little gap between her front teeth made her smile sexy. She reached her arms around his neck and kissed him. Her tongue was soft and warm.

"Except now I'm all grown up, and I'm a lot more fun. Race you to the car?"

She began running up the arroyo. Jeff checked out her hips. *Nice booty.* He tried to catch her, but he couldn't until she let him.

The contractor finished the remodel in a month. Emmy Lou had decided to paint the inside herself. She chose the colors. Jeff moved out of his apartment and into her house and helped her paint. He brought Budgey, and they kept his Wilson Hurley landscape and one little Steve Hanks nude. He sold the other nudes and paid down his credit cards. When the house was ready, Rachel and Ben and a couple of their friends came for a house warming. Jeff made hamburgers on the grill, Ben brought chips and dip, and the women made potato salad and cherry cheesecake. No one could stop laughing at Jeff's childish antics. He put his apron on backward, balanced a hamburger on his forehead, and Ben threw chips in the air so Jeff could catch them with his wide open mouth.

Emmy Lou excused everyone by nine so she and Jeff could go to bed early. "The doctor says Jeff needs his rest. Thanks for coming over." Emmy Lou took his hand and led him into the house. "Come on, Jeff, we've got thirty years of catching up to do."

Ben waved and grinned as everyone walked to their cars. "Rest well, Jeff, and keep your hive clean."

In the early morning, Jeff sat in a lawn chair with his coffee, watching the sunlight flood the foothills and a chipmunk scurry on the adobe wall. He felt peaceful as he watched the honey bees come and go from the two hives they had placed in the yard by the wall. Those little bees. They lived, built honeycomb, attended the queen, cleaned hives, and made honey for the future. They flew out of their hives unafraid, full of hope, eager for the next flower, gathered sweet nectar, and flew back, perhaps knowing that their service to the bee hive created a meaningful life. On a glide path to the hive, one honey bee slowed and hovered above Jeff. He looked up, tipped his head, and heard the murmur of God in the smooth wispy beating of wings. He was alive. He was grateful. He was home.

Readers Guide

1. This novel is an exploration of psychology, symbols, metaphors, and healing. The story follows a few years of Dr. Jeff Corley's life, and the antics and behavior of honey bees symbolize the forms of suffering Jeff endures. He gets "stung" by what he sets in motion in his own life. The ways of honey bees are metaphors for admirable behavior (protect the hive, serve others, build community). Ben reflects these metaphors back to Jeff. Is Ben's advice useful in Jeff's journey?

2. The theme of my novel is that we should never give up hope, and that love and compassion win out over a self-centered life style. Can you find the places where "there's always hope" is spoken? Hint: the first time is a blackjack dealer.

3. Each of the women (Rachel, Michelle, Veronica, Debbie, Elissa, and Emmy Lou) exhibit good ways of living with a narcissist. Can you find the healthy ways they choose? For example, after a troubled beginning, Rachel learns how to keep good boundaries and refuses to let him define her self-worth. Other ways include having an exit strategy, expecting and asking for cooperation, and expressing admiration only for what is truly admirable.

4. When Jeff meets and comes to know Michelle, he becomes obsessed with rearranging her body to suit his sense of how she should be. Think about the feelings you might have when someone tries to change you instead of loving you the way you are. Michelle finally got fed up and tried to rearrange Jeff. Can you blame Michelle for what she did?

5. As Jeff progresses through his relationships with women, he learns things from each of them that contributes to his ultimate transformation. Can you identify what he learns from each? For example, from Veronica, he learns the limitations of lust and physical pleasure, and from Rachel, he learns the joy of the steady presence of friendship. What did he learn from Debbie and her dying mother? What did he learn from Elissa? And finally, what did he learn from Emmy Lou?

6. The honey bees and the hive serve as symbols of the higher forms of life into which Jeff transforms. He starts out as utterly self-centered, selfish, and believing that life is all about him. The Hive, on the other hand, symbolizes community and the contributions to a higher cause. The bees exist to serve others and to be productive, the very opposite of Jeff's beginning. Can you find other symbols from the world of honey bees?

7. It seems that Jeff's character disorder came from his childhood tragedy and the need to escape who he was at that time. Think about the trauma he faced from blinding Emmy Lou. Does that trauma make his character more understandable?

8. Think about how Jeff finds his healing in his deepest wound. Do you think that might be true for most people? Do love and compassion often come from suffering?

www.ingramcontent.com/pod-product-compliance
Lightning Source LLC
Chambersburg PA
CBHW022137020726
47496CB00008B/2433